"Where *is* this guy? I just want to go to my hotel and sleep," Jessie groaned into her phone.

A man wearing an Australian version of a cowboy hat strode into the main terminal of the train station. He was tall, lean and rugged; his skin was tanned a deep golden brown, giving him the look of a man who spent his time outside working with his hands.

"Okay. Who are you looking at?" Valentina asked.

Jessie turned the phone around so her friend could see the man, who had stopped near the spot in the terminal where she had parked herself waiting for her brother's friend. He scanned the waiting areas until his eyes landed on her.

"Is *that* Bruce's friend?"

"Lord, I certainly hope so." Jessie's eyes were now locked with the man's striking light green eyes. She didn't look away and neither did he.

"When one door closes, another one opens to let a hot guy in," Valentina teased. "Call me later."

Jessie felt like a deer caught in headlights; she sat frozen while she waited for the man to reach her.

"Are you Jessie?" he asked with an Australian accent that sounded so sexy to her American ears.

"I am." She stood up and offered him her hand. "Are you Hawk?"

"At your service."

Dear Reader,

Thank you for choosing *Her Outback Rancher*, the sixteenth Harlequin Special Edition book featuring the Brand family. I am an unapologetic superfan of the *90 Day Fiancé* franchise and I have always known that I would incorporate a fiancé visa into a Brand book.

American cowgirl Jessie Brand, the youngest of eight and the only girl, was expected to take her place in the family horse breeding business but fate has other plans. On a trip to Australia, Jessie finds herself unceremoniously dumped by her long-term boyfriend, and on the train to Brisbane, she discovers that he has accidentally taken her backpack with her passport, leaving her with a backpack full of his dirty underwear. Luckily, her oldest brother, Bruce, has a friend in Brisbane who has agreed to pick her up at the train station and get her situated in her hotel. It never crossed Jessie's mind that her future would be walking through the train station doors.

Hawk Bowhill has outback cattle ranching in his blood. As the only grandson of a wealthy cattle baron, Hawk stands to inherit Daintree Downs, a sprawling cattle station in Queensland, Australia. Hawk isn't in the market for a relationship. But, the second he lays eyes on Jessie, Hawk knows that his life will never be the same. After disagreeing on what country to call home as a couple, a surprise pregnancy breaks the tie and Hawk agrees to move to Montana on a K1 Fiancé Visa. But blending in with Jessie's large, opinionated family is more difficult than he ever imagined...

I hope you love reading this book as much as I enjoyed writing it!

Happy reading,

Joanna

Her Outback Rancher
Rancher

———

JOANNA SIMS

HARLEQUIN
SPECIAL
EDITION

HARLEQUIN®
SPECIAL EDITION™

Recycling programs
for this product may
not exist in your area.

ISBN-13: 978-1-335-59424-2

Her Outback Rancher

For questions and comments about the quality of this book, please contact us at CustomerService@Harlequin.com.

Harlequin Enterprises ULC
22 Adelaide St. West, 41st Floor
Toronto, Ontario M5H 4E3, Canada
www.Harlequin.com

Printed in U.S.A.

Joanna Sims is proud to pen contemporary romance for Harlequin Special Edition. Joanna's series, The Brands of Montana, features hardworking characters with hometown values. You are cordially invited to join the Brands of Montana as they wrangle their own happily-ever-afters. And, as always, Joanna welcomes you to visit her at her website.

Books by Joanna Sims

Harlequin Special Edition

The Brands of Montana

The Montana Mavericks: Six Brides for Six Brothers

Visit the Author Profile page
at Harlequin.com for more titles.

Dedicated to the founding members
of my first (ever) book club:

Sarah Allred

Deborah Goodman

Brenda Stevens

Thank you for loving the Brand family as much as I do!

Prologue

"And then he took a shuttle to the airport and I haven't talked to him since," Jessie Brand told her best friend.

"Que idiota!" Valentina Flores-Cruz exclaimed.

"Si!" Video-chatting with her friend after her train arrived in Brisbane, Australia, it was the first time Jessie had felt like laughing since her boyfriend, Hudson, had left her. "He *is* an idiot. A total idiot. But, then again, so am I. I actually thought he was acting *off* because he was going to propose in the same place we had met several years ago. I couldn't have been further off base if I tried."

"You're not an idiot, Jess. You couldn't have known he was still talking to his ex-girlfriend."

"No." Jess had to agree. "And, I couldn't have

known that he would dump me in Sydney and head back to the States to be with her. It all still feels like a bad dream."

"I'm sure. How could it not?" Valentina said. "But, *do not* stalk them on social media, Jess. Resist the urge!"

"Too late," Jessie confessed.

"Glutton for punishment."

"I know," Jessie said. "Salt in the wound. He actually uploaded a video telling all of his 1,500 followers that he was flying back to his soulmate, his one true love."

"Idiota!" Valentina reiterated.

After the breakup brunch and after they had retrieved their bags from the concierge, Hudson took a taxi to the airport, and she took a shuttle to the Sydney train station. It wasn't until she was several hours into her trip that she realized that Hudson had accidentally taken her backpack. He had her passport and wallet and she had his backpack full of dirty socks and underwear. She was going to need to figure out how to get it back before she could leave the country. Now she was sitting in the Brisbane Roma Street Station waiting for a friend of her oldest brother, Bruce, to pick her up and take her to the hotel.

"You're better off," Valentina said bluntly. "I never liked him."

No one had really liked Hudson—not her family, not her friends. But despite that, she had loved him. Maybe it hadn't been the grand romance with all of the bells and whistles she had dreamed of as a little girl—but he had a genius IQ, shared her love of traveling and always knew how to make her laugh.

"Where *is* this guy?" Jessie suddenly felt exhausted. "I thought he would be here when I arrived. I just want to go to my hotel and sleep. I don't even know why I decided to come to Brisbane in the first place."

"Because you are obsessed with Steve Irwin, and you want to go see his zoo, that's why. You wouldn't be *you* if you let that *idiota* stop you."

Jessie was about to respond when a man wearing an Australian version of a cowboy hat, dark jeans and a neatly tucked button-down shirt strode into the main terminal of the train station. He was tall, lean and rugged; his skin was tanned a deep golden brown, giving him the look of a man who spent his time outside working with his hands. She was not the only woman in the building who noticed him; women were craning their necks every which way to get a better look at him. And she couldn't seem to take her eyes off him either. It was the way that he carried himself—self-assured and confident.

"Okay. Who are you looking at?" Valentina asked.

"An Aussie cowboy." Jessie flipped the camera around so her friend could see the man.

"Yes, please, Mr. Australian cowboy! Can you say, Hudson *who*?"

The man stopped near the spot in the terminal where Jessie had parked herself, waiting for Bruce's friend. The stockman looked at his phone and then looked around the station. He scanned the waiting areas until his eyes landed on her. The moment their eyes met, Jessie's heart began to beat faster, and she forgot to breathe for a split second.

"He's walking toward you," her friend said.

"He sure is." Jessie nodded, her heart fluttering in the most wonderful way.

"Is *that* Bruce's friend?"

"Lord, I certainly hope so."

Jessie's eyes were now locked with the man's striking light green eyes. She didn't look away and neither did he.

"When one door closes, another one opens to let a hot guy in," Valentina teased.

"I think I need to go."

"Call me later." Her friend ended the video call.

Jessie sat frozen while she waited for the man to reach her. His strides were long and determined; it felt like a split second, and he was standing in front of her.

"Are you Jessie?" he asked with an Australian accent that sounded so sexy to her American ears.

"I am." She stood up and offered him her hand. "Are you Hawk?"

"At your service." He lifted his hat politely, then shook her offered hand.

She slipped her hand into his large, callused, strong one. It reminded her of home and of the cattlemen in her family. "Thank you for coming to my rescue."

He picked up her two large bags, leaving only the backpack full of Hudson's laundry for her to carry.

"I hope it wasn't too much trouble."

"No worries," Hawk said. "Bruce is a mate."

They reached his sleek black Land Rover Defender; he opened the door for her, got her situated in the passenger seat and then loaded her bags into the SUV.

"Emporium Hotel?" he asked her when he joined her in the cab.

Jessie nodded, taking in the clean smell of Hawk's skin. The soap he used smelled like rum and cinnamon—a bit spicy and a bit sweet. Lovely. Every cell in her body seemed to be reacting to this Australian stockman; *all* of those elusive bells and whistles were suddenly going off! And why not? She was a free woman now, wasn't she?

"I got dumped," she blurted out.

"The bloke's obviously an idiot."

"That's what my friend just said!" Jessie exclaimed, partially with excitement for his compliment.

"So, what's next then?" he asked her as he pulled onto the road.

"Well—" she settled back in her seat "—my flight home isn't for two weeks. After I go to the zoo, I suppose I'll move my flight up and head back early. As long as my ex returns my passport, that is."

"Naw. You don't want to do that." Hawk glanced over at her with a broad, adorable smile.

She laughed at the way he said it—so direct, as if they had known each other all their lives. "I don't?"

"Of course you don't. Brissie's an awesome place," Hawk said, using the city's nickname. "I spend a lot of time here. You don't want to miss it. They have museums, botanical gardens. Kayaking. Pub crawl. Whatever you want. I'll be your tour guide." He smiled at her again. "We'll start with the zoo tomorrow."

"You want to be my tour guide?" She turned her body slightly in his direction, her arms crossed in front of her body.

"Of course I do," Hawk said without a moment's hesitation. "You're bloody gorgeous. Too gorgeous to be alone on your first night here. I'll take you to one of my favorite restaurants for dinner. Do you like Chinese food?"

She nodded, her mind whirling. It hadn't even been a full twenty-four hours since the breakup, and now she was having dinner with a handsome Australian cattleman? She certainly couldn't have predicted *that*!

"I'll take you to Donna Chang's. You'll love it."

"Did Bruce tell you to babysit me?" she asked, suddenly feeling a funny sensation in her stomach.

"No. He asked me to pick you up at the train station and make sure you got to the hotel safe. That's it."

"So, taking me out to dinner is your idea?"

"All my idea."

"You don't waste any time, do you?"

He gave her a quick wink with a confident smile. "A girl like you doesn't come around every day."

It was undeniable that this gorgeous man's unexpected interest in her took some of the sting out of being dumped in a foreign country by Hudson. Maybe a dinner date with a hot Aussie was *exactly* what she needed. And if dinner went well, maybe she would take him up on his offer to be her tour guide.

"So?" He prodded her out of her silence. "How about it? Do you want to come to dinner with me and see how we go?"

"Yes, Hawk," she said with her own smile. "I think I'd like that very much."

Brisbane was looking up.

Chapter One

One year later

"Hawk!" Jessie Brand shouted out her fiancé's name when she spotted him coming out of the terminal gate at the Bozeman International Airport.

Hawk's eyes found her, and he smiled in a way that always made her fall more deeply in love every time she saw him. She ran toward him full tilt and leapt into his arms, and he held on to her with one arm as he took several steps forward with her feet dangling in the air. Hawk stopped and dropped his bag so he could use both arms to wrap her up in a long-awaited hug.

"G'day, gorgeous," her outback rancher said, his lips finding hers.

"G'day, handsome." She laughed joyfully. It had been three long months since she had seen him in person; she had sorely missed his kisses.

Hawk put her down gently and didn't let go until her feet were safe on the ground. His eyes on her face, he put his hand over her tiny baby bump.

"How are you feeling?" he asked.

She put her hand over his. In a lowered, secretive voice, she said, "We're fine. I'm in perfect health and so is our baby."

He took her hand in his and kissed it sweetly. "That's all I needed to hear."

What Jessie had thought was a two-week rebound fling with a sexy Australian cowboy—only leaving reluctantly and after her ex Hudson had gotten her passport back to her—had turned into a yearlong cross-continental love affair. Hawk had flown her back to Australia several times over the past year, he had proposed marriage on her first return visit and she hadn't hesitated to say yes to him. As it turned out, Hudson dumping her had been a blessing. While he had returned to his soulmate, *she* had found *hers*, the man she wanted to spend the rest of her life loving. On her last trip to Australia, Hawk had given her the ultimate gift: a baby. Their lovemaking could be impulsive and impatient, and sometimes they were too hot to be bothered to take precautions. They hadn't necessarily planned the pregnancy, but they hadn't worked overtime to prevent it, and now they were both thrilled that their love had produced a child. She was about to enter her second trimester and her barely noticeable baby bump was soon going to be nearly impossible to hide from her family and friends.

"I can't believe that you're actually here." Jessie linked her arm with his as they made their way to baggage claim. "How was your flight?"

"Long but good."

Her fiancé pulled her close with his arm, and she melted her body into his.

"You'll fall in love with Montana, I promise."

She could hear the worry in her own voice; the biggest hurdle in their long-distance romance was answering the question "where do we live?" Hawk was the only grandson of a wealthy cattleman who owned one of the largest cattle stations in Australia. Hawk had been groomed from an early age to inherit Daintree Downs when his grandfather retired from the cattle business. Even when she began the K1 fiancé visa process for him to come to the United States, Hawk had been adamant that they build their lives together at Daintree Downs. But for Jessie, living on an isolated, nearly one-million-acre cattle station, where they needed to use a helicopter to visit the nearest neighbor, was not an option. She didn't want to homeschool their children, wait for their mail to be delivered by airplane or be half a day's drive away from civilization. She didn't want to spend her life without her family in close proximity, no matter how annoying they might be. The news of the baby had broken their stalemate, and Hawk agreed to come to Montana on the K1 visa. Jessie knew Hawk was giving up so much with life on the cattle station for her and their child; it only made her love him that much more.

He gave her a reassuring wink. "I already fell in love with Montana. I fell in love with you, didn't I?"

After they grabbed his bags, they headed toward her aqua blue Jeep Gladiator. While Hawk loaded his suitcases into the back seat of her truck, Jessie retrieved a present that she had left in the passenger seat.

"Welcome home." Jessie held out the present for Hawk to see.

Hawk shut the door firmly behind him as he looked at her gift: a black Stetson cowboy hat made in the American style.

He took his own hat off and placed it on her head; then he tried the Stetson on for size.

"Well?" he asked her.

"It's a perfect fit."

"You're a perfect fit." Hawk leaned down and gave her a kiss. "Thank you for the gift."

She put her hand over her growing belly. "Thank you for mine."

After they were situated in her truck, Jessie cranked the engine with a new set of butterflies in her stomach. As she pulled out on to the road, she said, "We only have ninety days to get married. Are you ready?"

"I've been ready to marry you since the first moment I saw you," he replied, then added in a teasing tone, "Now we're in a bit of a rush. You're pregnant— I've got to make an honest woman out of you."

Jessie slowed the truck as she approached Sugar Creek. She didn't want to use the main drive just in case someone spotted her. Instead, she cut through Little Sugar Creek, her brother Gabe's homestead, to access one of the many back roads on the ranch. Gabe, a long-distance horse hauler, was out on a job, and his wife, Dr. Bonita Delafuente-Brand, was at a medical conference in Washington, DC. So neither of them was on the property to spot her flashy Jeep. Of course, after all they'd heard about him, she was looking forward to introducing Hawk to her family and friends in person; many of her siblings and even her mom had met Hawk via video-chat. But after several failed attempts for Hawk to visit her in the States because of emergencies at Daintree Downs, she wanted him all to herself for his first couple of days in Montana.

"We have ten thousand acres," Jessie said, navigating a big dip in the road. "It's a lot smaller than Daintree Downs, but there's still quite a bit of elbow room."

"It's a real beauty," her fiancé said.

Jessie smiled at his compliment; the land of Daintree Downs was mostly flat and dusty from drought, with the occasional hill and patch of trees. Hawk had given her a bird's-eye view of the cattle station by helicopter. Jessie couldn't deny there was a raw, wild appeal to the land that had shaped the man she loved, but it just couldn't compare to the grassy prairies, acres upon acres of fine grazing pastures and majestic mountain ranges off in the distance, hallmarks of her beloved Sugar Creek Ranch. This was the land where she wanted her children to run free and explore as she had when she was a child. Once her wandering itch had been scratched after graduate school, Jessie realized that Sugar Creek was the place where she wanted to work, live, raise a family and grow old.

At a fork in the rough dirt road, Jessie stopped the Jeep and pointed. "Bruce and Savannah's homestead is just around that corner."

"I look forward to catching up with him," Hawk said. "I haven't seen him in years."

It was funny to think that they had Bruce to thank for their meeting. When Bruce, her eldest brother, was fresh out of college, their father, Jock, had sent him to Australia to study the different breeds of cattle being raised there and to purchase bull semen from Daintree Downs. That's when Bruce had first met Hawk, and they had been friends ever since, even though their busy lives often stopped them from talking regularly. For Jessie, their kinship made sense. Bruce and Hawk were both cowboys at their core. Ranch life was in their blood. And they both stood to inherit large, lucrative cattle properties at some point in their lives.

Jessie took the left fork in the road that would take them the back way to her brother Liam's cabin. Liam, a big animal veterinarian, was the second eldest of her seven older brothers. After he had married horse trainer Kate King, Liam had built his dream home on his wife's family ranch. His cabin was occasionally used for guests, but it hadn't been occupied for years, not since her brother Shane, a musician and veteran, had moved out. It would be the perfect spot for her to reconnect with Hawk before she introduced her family *officially* to her fiancé.

A fiancé her family didn't know she had. The family knew she was dating him, but she had decided to keep the pregnancy and the K1 visa private—until they had a chance to meet Hawk. She was the youngest of eight *and* the only girl. Her family was opinionated, loud and could be overbearing about everything in her life—especially her father, Jock. He was going to give Hawk a very hard time for getting his baby girl in the family way before asking him for her hand in marriage. Even though she was in her midtwenties, he still viewed her as the baby of the family. He didn't want her to marry too young, and he was suspicious of anyone who wasn't a cowboy from Montana.

It all came from a good place, but she was glad that Hawk was there in the flesh to wow her family in person. Even if she hadn't been entirely forthright about what her fiancé was walking into just yet…

"This is it." She parked the Jeep in front of the

cabin that Liam had built. The house was small with a wraparound front porch. There was a nearby barn that had been used for horses but had stood empty for several years. As far as Jessie knew, Liam still kept his vintage trucks in the large metal buildings across the clearing from the cabin, but with his busy practice and his life with Kate, Jessie imagined he rarely had time to come to Sugar Creek, which made this the perfect hideaway.

"This is a nice spot." Hawk stepped out of the Jeep and looked around the lush greenery that surrounded Liam's little oasis. "I could live here without much complaint, I'd imagine."

Jessie met Hawk at the front of the Jeep. "I love it here too."

Her fiancé seemed to be taking Montana in stride, but he'd only landed less than an hour ago. There hadn't been much time for him to truly absorb the fact that he was now in Montana after months of trying to convince her that she should move to Australia.

It was a huge change. How long would his good mood last? Could Hawk be happy making a life here in Montana with her?

"Let's grab the bags later," she suggested, slipping her hand into his.

Hawk was nobody's fool—he knew exactly what was on her mind. They hadn't made love in months, and her body ached for him. She always desired him—he was young and handsome and naturally sexy. Now that her pregnancy had thrown her libido into an entirely different gear, she couldn't wait to be skin to skin with Hawk, their limbs intertwined, their bodies joined.

Jessie used the hidden key in the nearby flowerpot to unlock the door. Hawk swung her into his arms, which made her laugh, and carried her over the threshold. He balanced on one leg so he could push the front door shut with his foot while still holding her firmly in his arms.

"That was a *super* sexy move, handsome." She nibbled on his ear.

"I was hoping that would turn you on." He let her down gently and then immediately pulled her into his warm embrace. He kissed her long and hard just how she liked, and her body started to purr just like a happy kitten.

With a mischievous smile on her lips, Jessie pushed away from her fiancé so she could untuck his shirt and unbutton it. Hawk watched her with a look that could only be read as pure desire. She pushed his shirt aside and ran her hands over his smooth chest.

"All you have to do is *breathe* and I get turned on."

"If you keep on doing that, it's going to be the floor for us." He captured her hand and kissed it. "Which way to the bedroom?"

"Straight ahead." She tugged her hand away playfully. "I'll race you!"

"What do I get when you lose?" He tried to recapture her hand but failed.

They were laughing loudly and bantering down the short hallway. Still in the lead, Jessie burst through the bedroom door, which had been half closed, raced into the room and launched herself onto the bed. Hawk had stripped off his shirt somewhere along the way and chased her, now bare-chested, into the bedroom.

"What in the actual *hell* is going on here?" Liam, who had been dozing on the bed, bolted upright, with a sleeping mask over his eyes. He tried to take off the mask several times before he finally ripped it off and threw it on the ground.

Shocked, Jessie bounced back up off the bed and faced her brother.

"What are you doing here, Liam?"

"Jessie?" Liam yanked earbuds from his ears and squinted at her as his eyes adjusted to the light. "The last time I checked, this is *my* cabin. What are *you* doing here?"

While Hawk shrugged his shirt back on and began to button it, Jessie was temporarily rendered speechless. Liam, still scowling, pointed at Hawk. "And who in the devil is *that*?"

"This is Hawk, my boyfriend."

Hawk raised up one hand in greeting. "Nice to meet you."

Her fiancé seemed to be moving toward Liam to shake his hand; she quickly blocked him with her arm. "We just came here to—"

"No," Liam cut her off as he stood up. "I get the picture."

"We didn't know you were here," she said.

"Apparently."

"I didn't see your work truck—"

"I parked it in the garage," Liam told her. "Not that it's any of your business what I do with my own truck on my own property."

Liam looked disheveled, and Jessie's brother *never* looked disheveled. His shirt was rumpled and un-tucked, he had stubble growing on his face and there were noticeable dark circles beneath his eyes. His blondish-brown hair, graying at the temples, was mussed. He looked exhausted and he was in a very bad mood.

"I'm sorry we barged in on you," she said, and meant it.

"I can't seem to find a minute of peace and quiet anywhere," Liam grumbled under his breath while he searched for his glasses on the nightstand. He found them, put them on and then stared hard at the both of them.

"Why don't we give you a minute to pull yourself together?" she said, slipping her hand into Hawk's. "I'll make us some coffee."

"Fine." Her brother sat down on the edge of the bed to yank on his boots. "Good."

Even though the cabin wasn't used often, Liam always kept nonperishable items, especially coffee, on hand.

"So—" Hawk stood stiffly near the small butcher-block kitchen island "—that's Liam."

She nodded as she scooped coffee into the filter. "Second oldest."

"He seemed surprised to see me here."

"Well, I didn't tell him we were coming. I just figured the place was empty. It usually is," she explained.

"I meant he seemed surprised to see *me*. In Montana. He didn't seem to have a bloody clue who I was or why I was here."

"Well, of course not." Jessie turned on the coffee pot with a shrug. "Liam has a flip phone, and he doesn't pay even one millisecond of attention to anything on social media. He knows I have an Australian boyfriend, of course. He was just surprised *in general*, that's all."

"Boyfriend? What happened to fiancé?" Now Hawk's eyes had turned a dark shade of green—a sure sign that he was *displeased* about something she had said or done. She had hoped to avoid this conversation with Hawk until at least the next morning, after they had made love four or five times.

"You know what I mean," she said, wishing that Hawk wasn't drilling down so hard on details at the moment. She was still trying to move past her disappointment over their derailed tryst. They should both be *naked* by now, not getting ready to have a heart-to-heart with her brother.

"No, I don't. It's a bit muddy on my end." Hawk

frowned at her. "Does your family even know that I'm here? Do they even know that we're engaged?"

"I have kept our *situation* on a need-to-know basis," she said as she took three coffee mugs out of the cabinet.

"How many needed to know?"

"Well…let me see." She put the mugs down on the island and pretended to count on her fingers. When she ran out of fingers, she looked at him directly and said, "That would be *two*."

Hawk stared down into Jessie's lovely face; she was half Chippewa Cree on her mother Lilly's side, which had given her golden skin, high cheek bones and thick, pin-straight black hair, which she wore long down to her waist. Her incredible ocean blue eyes came straight from her father Jock's Scottish heritage.

"Two?" He leaned forward a bit and lowered his tone. "As in only two people know I'm here? Or as in only two people know that we're engaged?"

"Both."

"You have seven brothers, seven sisters-in-law, umpteen cousins, nieces and nephews, and only *two people* know?"

"I just said that, didn't I?" Jessie's tone had a definite snap in it.

Hawk could tell by the set of Jessie's jaw and her body language that his questions were starting to annoy her just as much as her responses were provoking him. Two quick tempers lighting aflame.

"Well, make that four. Bruce and Savannah had to sponsor you for the K1 visa. They were the only two people in my family who *really needed to know*!"

Of course, he remembered that Bruce had to sponsor him, because Jessie didn't have enough of a financial history to bring him to the States on her own. He hated it. And frankly, despite the positive demeanor he'd adopted since stepping off the plane, if there hadn't been a baby, he wouldn't have agreed to move to the States.

"I think you may be missing my point," he countered. "Does anyone know about our baby?"

Jessie pressed her lips together, a signal to him that she didn't want to discuss it further. Hawk clamped his mouth shut so he could keep himself from saying anything that would drag them both into a fight in front of one of Jessie's brothers. That wouldn't help their cause at all. In front of her family and friends, many whom would no doubt be skeptical of his intentions, they needed to present a united front.

The truth was he already knew the answer to his question about their unborn child. If the majority of her large, extended family had no idea that they had to get married in ninety days, they certainly didn't know that they were expecting a child. He didn't approve of keeping her family in the dark; he had been so busy with what was happening in Australia, he hadn't even thought to ask Jessie about her family. For him, this was a real punch in the gut.

What was he walking into?

There was an uncomfortable silence between them when Liam emerged from the bathroom looking refreshed, with his shirt tucked in neatly and his hair slicked back off his face.

"Come here, you." Liam opened his arms for Jessie, seemingly unaware of the tension in the room.

Jessie hugged her brother tightly. "You're hiding from the wedding posse, aren't you?"

"Guilty as charged," Liam said with a small, sheepish smile. "All the women in my life have got wedding fever. They're at it morning, noon and night. I go to sleep, and all I see is lace and ribbons and wedding invitations and wedding dresses, cake toppers and tiaras. It's a living hell."

Jessie explained for Hawk's benefit. "Liam's daughter, Callie, is getting married."

"Cheers, mate," Hawk said.

"Thank you, Hawk." Liam held out his hand to him. "Let's try this again. It's nice to finally meet you. I've heard a lot about you from Bruce and Jessie."

"Likewise." Jessie's brother's handshake was firm but welcoming, and despite their rocky introduction, Hawk took an immediate liking to him.

They took their coffee to the living room. Liam sat

in a rocking chair near the fireplace while he joined Jessie on an overstuffed two-seater couch. Hawk appreciated the floor-to-ceiling wall of windows that provided an unfettered view of distant mountains. It wasn't his beloved Australian outback, but he had to admit that this was beautiful country.

After Liam took a sip of his coffee, he put the mug on the end table and said, "So, fill me in."

After a second or two of silence, Liam prodded his sister. "Come on, Jess. I know I'm out of the loop, but Kate's not. Heck, Kate *is* the loop most of the time. I didn't hear one word about Hawk coming here for a visit, yet here he is." Liam raised an eyebrow at his sister. "And no one comes to my hideaway unless they're trying to avoid the family."

Hawk gave her hand a squeeze, and he supposed it gave her the extra little push she needed to lay it out straight for Liam.

"Hawk is here on a K1 fiancé visa, I'm pregnant, and we have ninety days to get married."

Hawk was surprised that Jessie hadn't even attempted to sugarcoat the situation for her brother. Her response had been blunt and direct, with a large dose of pride and determination.

Liam didn't respond right away; he took another sip of his coffee, rocked in his chair and then said, "Well, congratulations and *crikey*. Isn't that what Australian's say in moments like these? *Crikey?*"

"Don't say *crikey*, Liam," Jessie said. "It sounds weird when you say it."

"He can say *crikey*," Hawk defended Liam. "That was a perfect use of *crikey*."

"Well, his wife won't like it, and she'll tell him to stop." Jessie curled her legs up next to her on the couch, seeming more relaxed now that she had told Liam their secret.

Liam laughed easily. "She's right. Kate will hate it, and that will be the end of it for me, I'm afraid."

"Feel free to use it anytime when we're together." Hawk played along. "I'll be your safe space."

"You know what, Jess?" Liam said. "I really like this guy. He's good people."

"Okay," Jessie said to them both, "I'm super glad that the two of you have already bonded and apparently started a bromance in the span of fifteen minutes. That's super cool. Let's pray that things go this easily with Pop."

"Well, that's another problem entirely, now isn't it?" Liam asked, his joking demeanor shifting to a more serious one. "You'd better think long and hard about how you're going to approach Pop with all of this, Jess. You're his only daughter and—" he nodded his head in the general direction of her belly "—first came the baby and then came the marriage isn't going to sit well with Jock Brand, now is it? We don't want Hawk here to meet the unfriendly end of one of Jock's antique Colt Peacemakers."

Hawk's smile faded completely. "Is Jock a good aim?"

"He's a crack shot," Liam told him.

Jessie nodded her head agreement.

Hawk had faced many a wild scrub bull on his land without fear, but facing Jessie's father was another thing entirely. "Well, *crikey.*"

Chapter Two

"Happy?" Hawk was laying on his back propped up on pillows, one arm behind his head and the other holding her tight.

"So happy." Jessie had her head resting on his bare chest with her arm wrapped around his torso. Her leg was draped over his thigh.

With Liam's blessing, they had hidden away in his cabin and spent several days lounging, talking, reconnecting and making love. They had made love so many times that she finally felt satiated and relaxed.

She could feel her fiancé smile just before he kissed the top of her head.

"It's time to emerge from our little love nest." Jessie ran her pointer finger along the defined ridges of his abs. "Face the music with the folks."

"You're right."

She tilted her head upward so she could look at his face. "Are you ready to meet the in-laws?"

"I'm ready," Hawk said definitively. "Are they ready for me?"

He'd had several days of rest now, and they had—in between lovemaking, sleeping and eating—discussed her decision to keep their impending marriage a secret. He didn't really agree with how she'd handled it, but Jessie knew that Hawk had come to terms with it.

"It might be a bit rough in the beginning, but they'll come around eventually," she said, looking down at the naked ring finger on her left hand. When Hawk proposed marriage, he had told her that he wanted to give her his grandmother's engagement ring. It was a family heirloom, and he felt that it was rightfully hers as the mother of the next generation of Bowhills.

Hawk must have seen her looking at her ringless finger, because he said, "I'm sorry that I couldn't bring the ring with me."

Jessie didn't respond right away, because the thought of his grandfather refusing to give him the ring hurt. She had always thought that Hawk's grandfather, William, liked her. But families were complicated.

"Do you ever think he'll accept me?" she finally asked.

"Hey," Hawk said, lifting her chin and looking

down into her eyes, "my grandfather accepts you. What he can't accept is my decision to move here."

"Will he ever?"

"I don't know," Hawk said honestly. "I have to believe that he will. Given enough time."

Satisfied for the moment, Jessie snuggled down into Hawk's embrace, and they held each other, enjoying these final moments of peace between them. Knowing that they couldn't stall any longer, Jessie pushed herself upright, and the sheet fell away from her body, leaving her breasts bare. Hawk naturally reached out to cup one in his hand and run his thumb over the nipple.

"Hmm." She closed her eyes for a minute. Then she caught his hand, kissed it as he often did hers and smiled at him with her eyes. "Later, handsome. We have to get ready for Sunday brunch. Everyone's expecting us."

Jessie had called her mother, Lilly, to let her know that Hawk had come for a visit and that he would be joining them for family brunch. After brunch, she had promised Hawk that they would have the chance to speak with her parents privately. For Hawk, it was imperative that Jock and Lilly understand the full scope of why he was here—the marriage, the baby, his relocation, all of it.

Jessie slipped out of bed, walked around to his side, pulled the sheet off Hawk's body and held out her hand for him.

"Care to join me for a shower?"

Hawk's eyes drank her body in before he sat up, ignored her hand, pulled her forward by taking her hips in his hands and kissed her small baby bump.

"Care for a quickie?" her fiancé asked.

Laughing, Jessie wiggled away. "No! We already had a quickie. We can't have a post-quickie quickie."

"I don't think that's a rule."

Jessie walked into the bathroom and turned on the water. "It's gonna be hot."

Hawk followed behind her, completely comfortable in his nakedness. "That's how I like it."

She let her fiancé get into the shower first; it was a small shower, barely room for two, but they made it work. Hawk soaped up his chest, and then Jessie used the soap to wash his back. She gave him a little pat on his firm backside when she was done with her chore. He turned around; instead of taking the soap from her, he wrapped his arms around her and kissed the droplets of water from her neck, her cheeks and her lips.

"No, sir!" Jessie pushed on his chest playfully. "We *cannot* be late for brunch. Not today of all days."

The house that Jock Brand had built for his family was massive. The outside was made from logs harvested from Sugar Creek land and there were three main wings. When Jessie parked her Jeep in the gravel area where several other trucks were parked, she pointed to the wing on the far right.

"That's where my suite of rooms is located." She

shifted into Park and shut off the engine. "Even though I'm still technically living with my parents, my suite is two stories, and I have my own kitchenette. I told them I was staying with a friend for the last few days."

"Is this the apartment you arranged for us?" Hawk asked, realizing that there were many conversations they had failed to have prior to his arrival. The K1 visa had been approved prior to the pregnancy; when he found out the news that they were expecting, there was only one month left of the six-month window to enter the US post visa approval.

"Well—" Jessie gave him a sheepish look "—*arranged* might be a strong word."

Hawk took in a deep breath to calm his nerves and to push down a rising sense of frustration with the entire process. Jessie had definitely left out some important details about their lives on the ranch; of course, Hawk had to remind himself, it wouldn't have changed anything. He would not have his first-born child brought into this world without him.

Jessie put her hand on his and squeezed it. "I'll take you to the hundred acres that is set aside for me. For us."

Hawk kissed her hand. "I'd like that."

Jock Brand had sired eight children from two different women. His first wife had been Scottish, and she and Jock had had four sons before she died. Jock's second wife, Lilly Hanging Cloud, had borne more sons and one daughter. Lilly was a member of the Chippewa Cree Tribe, was raised on the Rocky Boy Reservation. From what Jessie had told him, Jock was a gruff but fair man who had always dreamed of having all eight of his children living on homesteads on Sugar Creek.

Jessie met him at the front of her Jeep. "I'll ask Liam if we can crash at his cabin until we can build a home of our own."

Wordlessly, Hawk offered his fiancée his arm. He was nervous again; he hated that feeling. The sooner they let Jessie's family know about the ninety-day deadline, the marriage and their baby, the better. Hawk wasn't one for secrets.

Jessie held on to his arm as they advanced up the stone walkway that lead to the front door of Jock's log cabin mansion. In the foyer, Hawk could see the craftsmanship employed in order to carve out the deep filigree patterns in the tall double wood doors.

"How many of your brothers are going to be here today?" Hawk asked. It was rare that he felt reluctant to meet people, but the idea of sitting down with Jessie's parents and her seven siblings unnerved him. He didn't like the feeling.

"Bruce will be there—you already know him, so that's fine. Savannah, his wife, will be there as well—you've video-chatted with her, so no biggie. And Liam will be there."

"That's not insurmountable."

"Of course not," Jessie tried to reassure him. "So,

really, you only have to meet Gabe, Hunter, Colt, Noah and Shane."

"Just five more."

"And their wives, of course."

"Of course."

"*And* their kids."

Hawk nodded his head but the tension in his body, particularly his shoulders and neck, made it difficult for him to lighten his mood.

"Hey," Jessie said, looking up at him, "it's going to be fine. Dad might scream, curse and then give me the silent treatment for a few days. But he always forgives me."

"He might forgive *you*," Hawk said, nodding his head toward the door to signal that he was ready to face his new family. "I suspect I would fall into an entirely different category."

"Give me a kiss for luck." Jessie tilted her head back and puckered her full, naturally rosy lips.

"I thought we didn't need luck," he said.

"Just kiss me, Hawk." Her lips turned down into a little frown that had always made him laugh. He imagined that that little frown had gotten Jock to move mountains for his only daughter.

He leaned down and pressed his lips firmly to hers. When he broke the kiss, Hawk realized that he did feel a smidge better.

Jessie opened the front door, and Hawk was met with an enormous entryway that boasted an incredible vaulted ceiling, beautifully polished floors and thick tree trunks used as pillars.

"Everything you see here was sourced from Sugar Creek. Dad flew in artisans to complete the work."

"Impressive."

Taking his arm again, Jessie smiled up at him, her bright blue eyes shining with love and excitement. Perhaps she was just naive; he couldn't imagine that the response from her parents, and perhaps some of her siblings, would be a cause for excitement.

"I'm so proud to be on your arm, Pengana." Jessie rarely used his given name, but he loved hearing it. Like Jessie, he also had indigenous heritage.

Hawk's mother was a member of the First Peoples in Australia, whose tribe lived in the Northern Territory of Australia. Hawk's father, William Bowhill Jr., had gone to the Northern Territory to gain experience in the cattle business. He'd brought more than just that experience back to Daintree Downs; Junior had returned with a wife who was pregnant with their first and, as it turned out, only child. Even though William Sr. was against the match, he embraced his grandson but never called him by his given name. Instead, William Sr. called him Hawk, which was a loose translation of *Pengana* in English.

The name Hawk had stuck; his mother was the one person who still used his given name. When Jessie said it, it gave him both comfort and confidence.

"Miss Jessie!" A short heavyset woman appeared in the entryway, her brown-black hair cut into a blunt bob that framed her round face, the gray at her temples uncolored. She appeared to be in her late fifties, early sixties. Her no-nonsense walk, Hawk noticed, matched her no-nonsense hair. "Two more minutes and you would have been late."

"I know," Jessie said. "We cut it close."

"Too close," the housekeeper said.

After Jessie introduced Hawk to Maria, the housekeeper said, "Now scoot. Brunch is about to be served."

"Thank you, Maria," Jessie thanked Maria and gave her a quick hug.

Maria hung Hawk's new Stetson on a nearby hook. Out of the corner of his eye, he saw the head housekeeper point to him when she said to Jessie. *"Muy guapo."*

"Yes." Jessie laughed and squeezed his arm playfully. "He *is* very handsome."

"Finally!" Jock Brand frowned at her.

Jessie wrapped her arms around her father's neck and kissed his cheek. Years of working in the Montana sun had turned his once fair skin leathery and wrinkled, with a ruddy undertone. His weathered skin was a sharp contrast to his deep-set, shocking, intelligent aquamarine eyes and snow-white hair, which he wore combed back off his heavily lined forehead.

"We are right on time, Dad," Jessie said. "I love you."

"I love you, baby girl," Jock grumbled the words, but the scowl on his face had softened.

"Good morning, mama." Jessie hugged her mom quickly so she could get back to Hawk's side.

"Dad, Mama, I'd like to introduce you to Hawk Bowhill."

"Hawk." Jock stood up and offered his hand for a brief shake. "Welcome to Sugar Creek."

"Thank you, sir. It's beautiful country here."

Jock gave a quick nod of his head before he sat back down. For Jessie, this initial meeting between Jock and her fiancé was a resounding success.

Lilly had stood up and rounded the table to greet Hawk. "It's a pleasure to have you here with us."

"Thank you, I'm happy to be here with you," Hawk said. Jessie was sure that her mother would respond to Hawk's kind heart and polite ways. He had been raised a gentleman.

Bruce stood up, came around the table and gave Hawk a hug and pat on the back. "Welcome to Montana, brother! As soon as you're ready, we've got plenty of work for you to do."

"Thank you, Bruce." Hawk had a look of genuine affection and respect for Jessie's eldest brother. For her, it was the exact stamp of approval she needed to assuage any issues Jock may have about her plan to marry her overseas boyfriend in the span of ninety days.

"Hawk!" Bruce's wife, Savannah, had also come

around the table to welcome him to the family brunch. "It's good to finally meet you in person!"

Hawk and Bruce had mainly kept in touch via text, video chat or social media. This was the first opportunity for Savannah to meet Hawk in the flesh.

"Good to see you again." Liam raised his hand in a friendly wave. "I'm afraid that you won't get to meet my wife, Kate, or my daughter, Callie. The wedding."

"The wedding," Hawk said with a small smile of understanding.

"And our daughter, Amanda, is with Kate and Callie," Savannah said, retaking her seat before she tossed part of her thick sorrel-red mane of hair over her shoulder. "She's the flower girl."

Bruce and Liam exchanged a look and said in unison, "The wedding."

After everyone was seated, Maria, who, as always, had been standing just outside the dining room doorway waiting for an opportune moment, asked, "Are we ready to serve?"

"Yes, please." Lilly smiled affectionately at Maria.

"You know what, baby girl?" Jock's eagle eyes drilled in on her face, and he had one bushy white eyebrow cocked upward. "It's mighty interesting to me that Liam had a chance to meet this young man before I did."

Jessie took the seat to her father's right. Usually, Savannah would take this spot as Jock's favorite daughter-in-law. But Bruce's wife was well versed in the family dynamics, and she had left that seat open for Jessie.

Jessie leaned forward, propped her chin on her head and gave her father her full attention. Her body position was deliberately teasing. "Why is that mighty interesting, Dad?"

Three cooks and Maria carried platters and bowls of scrambled eggs, bacon, sausage, toast with jams, grits, hash browns and pancakes. There was something for everybody.

The food put a temporary pause on Jock's line of questioning. Once he had eaten, he'd be a touch more reasonable. Everyone knew that.

"So, Hawk—" Jock stabbed a sausage Maria had put on his plate "—Liam has been telling us all about you."

Jessie stopped chewing and glanced at her brother quickly, and he gave an almost imperceptible shake of his head. Liam hadn't spilled the beans.

"But there's one question I had that nobody at this table could answer for me, but you…"

"Sir?"

Jock took the time to chew his sausage while Hawk waited for his next words. Jock swallowed and then used his fork to point at her fiancé. "How long are you staying with us?"

Jessie knew that Jock would have some pointed questions for them—that was his way—but this was a question that she had hoped wouldn't come up. She was about to respond, when Hawk, surprisingly, said, "Well, sir, I hope to discuss my plans with you after we eat."

Jock dropped his elbows on the table, leaning way forward, his laser-focused blue eyes on Hawk. "I certainly hope that you're not going to be asking for my daughter's hand in marriage. Baby girl here is too young to hitch her wagon to anybody."

Everyone at the table, everyone except for Lilly, was looking at Jock, no doubt hoping he wasn't about to go off on a tangent that would ruin the peace in the house.

Jock gave a shake of his head, broke the eye contact with Hawk and leaned back with a little laugh while he stabbed another sausage. He held up the sausage, inspected it and then said, as if talking to himself, "No, sir. I sure hope you weren't going to ask me that."

"Jock." Lilly gave her husband *the look*.

"All right, all right." Jock sat back a bit and flashed a sheepish smile in his wife's direction. "My wife here thinks I'm ruining the meal in front of company, Hawk. Am I ruining it for you?"

"Well, you're ruining it for me," Jessie answered. "I think that should count for something."

Hawk had his forearms resting on the edge of the table, his hands still holding his empty fork and knife over the plate. He looked Jock right in the eye. "No, sir, you haven't ruined anything for me. I appreciate the opportunity to come to your beautiful home and meet Jess's family."

Jock took a big bite of grits that had been swimming in butter, salt and pepper. After he swallowed, he hit the table again with his fist and then pointed at Hawk. "Now you see there? That's some good upbringing right there."

Lilly managed to steer the conversation to Callie's wedding, which gave Jock plenty of time to indulge in all of his favorite breakfast fare. Jessie did notice that her father had aged more quickly over the last several years, and his belly was now hanging way over his belt. No matter how many times the family *and* his doctor lectured, educated or cajoled him, Jock refused to slow down on fatty foods, red meat, cigars or whiskey—not necessarily in that order.

"Well," Savannah said, her face glowing in a way that drew Jessie's attention, "Bruce and I have some news."

Jock pushed his plate forward, signaling to the cook hovering nearby that he was finished. The cook quietly cleared Jock's plate away.

Bruce smiled affectionately at his wife; he had so much love in his blue eyes for Savannah even after they had been married for many years and had been through so much tragedy. Jessie reached for Hawk's hand; she only hoped that she would have the enduring love with Hawk that Bruce had found with Savannah. They were truly a match made in heaven and proof that if there is enough love, a couple could endure just about anything together.

"Do you want to tell them?" Savannah asked a bit shyly. Her dark emerald green eyes were sparkling with a secret.

"No." Her brother squeezed his wife's hand. "The floor is yours, sweetheart."

Before Savannah began talking, a thought came into Jessie's head. She locked eyes with her friend and sister-in-law. "No?"

Jessie put her hand over her mouth, doing her very best not to blurt out the riddle she had just solved.

Liam pointed at Jessie. "I was thinking the exact same thing!"

"Well, let her tell it," Lilly said, her face expectant as she looked at Savannah. Even though Lilly was their stepmother by law, none of Jessie's four older brothers thought of her as anything other than Mom. And Jessie had never thought of them as half brothers. They were just her brothers.

"You all know what a long journey we've been on to conceive," Savannah said, her voice trembling slightly with emotion. She looked at her husband. "We wanted to add to our family so desperately. And we didn't want Amanda to be an only child. That's not how the Brands do it…"

Jock leaned forward with his forearms resting on the table and his hands balled together. "Are you trying to tell me that we've got another grandbaby on the way?"

Savannah had some fresh tears rolling down her cheeks, and Bruce quickly took his cloth napkin to gently dry the tears on his wife's face.

"We're pregnant," Savannah said, beaming. "We are going to be blessed with another child."

Chapter Three

Jessie chimed in with the rest of the table to offer Bruce and Savannah her congratulations. Her brother and sister-in-law had one daughter together but had always wanted to expand their family.

After everyone else had taken a turn hugging Savannah and shaking Bruce's hand, overcome with excitement, Jessie raced around the table and sat down in the empty chair beside Savannah.

"How far along are you?" she asked.

"Three months. I wanted to wait until I got through the first trimester..." Savannah's voice trailed off. Because Savannah had suffered two miscarriages, Jessie understood why her sister-in-law had wanted to wait until she had reached that second trimester milestone before sharing the news.

"I can't believe this!" Jessie took her sister-in-law's hand in hers. "Our kids will be the same age, Savannah! They'll grow up side by side right here on Sugar Creek!"

Minutes after Jessie had blurted out that she was pregnant, Sunday brunch ended on an awkward note. In the aftermath, Jessie had sent Hawk a horrified, apologetic look, but to her surprise, his face was completely calm. Even his shoulders were more relaxed than they had been earlier in the brunch.

"It's going to be okay," Liam whispered to her as he gave her a huge, brotherly hug. Ever the diplomat, Liam shook Hawk's hand before he headed out.

In the short time from confession to Liam taking his leave, Jock and Lilly hadn't spoken a single word. In all her life, Jessie had never seen Jock so furious that he was rendered speechless. Her father's face had turned a deep shade of red up into his hairline, contrasting severely with his white hair. Purple splotches scorched his cheeks.

Her mom, who had always stood between the children and Jock's explosive temper, was sitting as still as a statue. In her mother's dark brown eyes, Jessie saw complete disappointment. Being the only girl in the family, Jessie had never kept a secret from Lilly; her first transgression was a worst-case scenario.

Bruce and Savannah didn't move from their spots, Jock still didn't know the whole of the situation, and

Jessie had to believe that they were staying in order to take some of the heat off her and Hawk.

Finally, after a long silence, where the only audible sound was Jock grinding his teeth, Lilly took her husband's hand in hers and asked in a steady voice, "Is there anything else you need to tell us?"

Jessie held Hawk's hand tightly, as much for her own comfort as it was for his. She exchanged a look with Hawk, and in that moment of nonverbal communication, Jessie knew that her fiancé wanted the bandage ripped off the rest of the way.

"Hawk is here on a K1 fiancé visa," Jessie said, her voice wavering from the adrenaline pumping through her body.

Jock had been drilling a hole in the oak table with his eyes, but when she mentioned the word *fiancé*, her father turned his gaze to her face. Still not speaking a word, the redness on his face traveled down his neck.

"And what does that mean exactly?" Lilly asked, holding tight to her husband's hand.

"It means that we have ninety days to get married, or Hawk will have to return to Australia."

Her mother's pretty face registered both surprise and disappointment.

"I think you should fill us in, Jessie," Lilly said.

Jessie glanced at Bruce, well aware of the fact that she had dragged her brother into a huge mess. At the time, she had been certain that keeping the K1 Visa and her pregnancy a secret was the best decision. Now, she could plainly see that she had been wrong.

"I sponsored him, Pop," Bruce said. As the oldest and the heir apparent of the Sugar Creek holdings, Bruce had grown into his role as "Jock whisperer" over the years.

"Sponsor him?" Lilly asked.

"I've only been collecting a paycheck for a year," Jessie said. After she had returned from Australia, she had been put in charge of the quarter horse breeding program; but her salary for only one year wasn't enough to sponsor Hawk on her own.

"So, you knew about this?" Jock asked his eldest child after stewing silently.

"Yes, I did."

"You helped them," Jock added.

Bruce nodded.

There was a rather long, uncomfortable silence before Jock asked Bruce, "And you didn't think to tell your mother or me?"

"It wasn't for me to tell, Pop," Bruce replied calmly. "When I found out there was a baby involved, I helped them. I'd like to believe you would have done the same if you were in my shoes."

"We'll never know, now will we?" Jock pressed his palms flat on the table.

"No," Bruce agreed, "I suppose we won't."

"This is a lot for us to process," Lilly said quietly, her eyes locked with Jessie's. "You're pregnant and you have to be married in ninety days?"

Red splotches of red dotted her father's neck and cheeks. After another couple of awkward seconds ticking by, Jock shook his head. "I welcomed you into my home and I wouldn't expect this. Not from either one of you."

"I'm sorry, Dad. Mom." Jessie couldn't figure out how to fix the mess she had made. "Keeping all of this a secret was my idea. Hawk didn't know about any of it until he arrived."

"I expect better of you, baby girl. I really do." Jock crossed his arms over his chest, his eyes fixed on scenery outside the floor-to-ceiling windows. Then Jock turned his gaze to Hawk. "Bowhill, I believe we're overdue for a talk."

Hawk nodded and he seemed so much calmer than she felt inside. "Yes, sir."

Jock stood up, pushed his chair out of his way and marched with a heavy foot out of the dining room. Hawk stood up and so did she.

"Jessie," Lilly said, "if you want any of this to work out, you can't be a shield for Hawk," Lilly said. "They need to find their own way, or your father will never respect him. Your father will never accept him."

"But, this was my mistake, not his."

"And you've apologized," Lilly said.

Hawk gave her a quick kiss. "Your mother's right. This, I have to do alone."

"I'm sorry." She hugged him tightly. "Not my finest hour."

"What's done is done," Hawk said. "Don't get all stressed out. It's not good for you or the baby."

"Bowhill!" Jock yelled from the foyer.

"It's going to be okay," Hawk tried to reassure her. "The worst is over."

Jessie wanted to believe her beloved, but Hawk didn't know Jock. In her experience, the scene in the dining room was just a preview of the worst that was yet to come.

Hawk followed Jessie's father to his office, which reflected the man's need to display his success in life. The office was large and masculine, decorated heavily with carved dark wood, fine rugs and high-end leather. Jock sat down behind his massive desk; Hawk sat down in one of the chairs at the front of the desk. The office had been decorated in a way that emphasized the importance that Jock placed on his family, his wealth and his success. Pictures of his children and grandchildren held a prominent place on his desk, the textured walls and the floor-to-ceiling bookcases. A nearly life-size painting of Lilly and a young Jessie in traditional Chippewa Cree regalia set in a fancy gold frame was the only decoration in the wall space directly behind the desk.

Jock stared Hawk down while he rocked back and forth in his leather-tooled executive chair.

"I had hoped to share our news with you and your wife privately." Hawk finally broke the silence between them.

Jock tapped his fingertips together several times. "It didn't work out that way."

"No, sir, it sure didn't."

Jessie's father continued to glare at him while Hawk searched his brain for the exact wording to right this capsized boat. From the look on the man's face, Hawk had little doubt that Jock would like to put some buckshot in his hide and send him packing back to Australia.

"I—*we*—planned to speak to you after brunch."

Jock rocked back in his chair with a stony expression on his face. "Speak now or forever hold your peace, Bowhill. But I give you fair warning, I don't believe what you're about to say is gonna change my mind one iota about this situation we're in."

Hawk bristled at his words. His shoulders stiffened, and his jaw clenched, but he forced himself to breathe in a couple of calming breaths before speaking.

"I love your daughter." Hawk thought that this was the only place to start.

"Of course you do."

"And she loves me."

Jock jerked forward in his chair. "Jessie's young. What does she know about love? One minute she's gallivanting all over Europe and Australia with that neutered lapdog, Hanson…"

"Hudson."

"I don't give a damn what his name is—he wasn't good enough for my baby girl!" Jessie's father snapped.

"And now I get *you*? Lilly told me you were the rebound."

"May I ask—" Hawk worked hard to keep his tone even and his voice calm "—what is your objection to me?"

Jock's forearms landed heavily on the desk as he leaned forward. "What is my *objection*?"

"Yes, sir," he said. "What is your objection?"

Jessie's father pointed at him with his middle finger again. "Let's start with the fact that you got my daughter in a family way without the benefit of marriage."

Hawk cringed inwardly. He couldn't blame anyone else; passion had overruled reason, and now he had to face Jessie's father. Jock was old-fashioned, and even though he didn't have much of a leg to stand on in this area, so was he.

"I came here with every intention of marrying Jessie. I love her and can assure you that I will provide for your daughter and our child."

"*Provide* for her?"

"Yes, sir."

"*Provide* for her? Jessie is more than capable of providing for herself. Do you know she's one of the most talented quarter horse breeders and trainers I've ever seen? We've got people from all over the world on waiting lists for Sugar Creek foals."

"I only meant that I want to be Jessie's partner and a good father for our child."

"Why are you really here?" Jock seemed to brush

aside his response while he looked at him through squinted examining eyes. "Are you after a green card? Is that it?"

Hawk tried to reply, but Jock kept going.

"Whatever you were looking for, you ain't gonna find it here. My advice? Get on the next plane home and find yourself a nice Australian *sheila*. You're not the one for my Jessie."

Hawk cleared his throat. "I would like your permission to marry your daughter, sir."

"Hell, no."

Hawk stood up. "I would have preferred to have your blessing."

"When hell freezes over." Jock stabbed the desk with his finger. "Or when pigs fly. Take your pick."

"I need you to understand that I am going to marry Jessie with or without your blessing."

Jock stood up as well—his face, neck and scalp turning blotchy with shades of red and purple. "Who in tarnation do you think you are? You come to *my* house on *my* land and tell me what you're gonna do with *my* daughter? You've got one hell of a nerve, Bowhill! One hell of a damn nerve!"

Convinced that he had hit a dead end with Jock, Hawk headed toward the door. At the closed door, he paused. He turned around to face Jessie's father.

"I hope one day we can sit down and hash this out, sir. For Jessie's sake."

Jock sprung up out of his chair, still scowling, and bellowed, "Cold day in hell, Bowhill."

* * *

"I am so sorry, Savannah," Jessie said to her sister-in-law. "I ruined your big announcement."

Savannah was sitting closely to Bruce, while he had his arm draped over the back of her chair.

"Don't worry about it, Jess." Savannah reached for her husband's hand. "Nothing could spoil how blessed we feel."

"Still—" she wound strands of her long, black hair around her finger "—I wish I had a Rewind button."

The four of them—Savannah, Bruce, her mother, and Jessie—were sitting around the big dining table, cleared of the dishes now. Her mother had been quiet, which wasn't a surprise. Lilly always was thoughtful and methodical when it came to conflicts in the family.

During a lull in their conversation, Jock's booming voice reached them. Lilly looked in the direction of her husband's office, her lips drawn down, before she turned her attention back to her.

"That doesn't sound good," Jessie remarked, her stomach twisting into a tighter, more painful knot.

"Your father loathes surprises," her mother said.

"I know." Jessie nodded.

"This could have been handled better," Lilly added.

"I know."

"Then, why wasn't it handled better?"

Jessie fiddled with a loose thread on the armrest of her chair. After a second or two, she said, "I guess

I didn't want to deal with Dad for obvious reasons. Nothing is ever easy with him. So I figured once Hawk was here and once Dad saw what a great guy he is, the rest would just fall into place."

Lilly breathed in through her nose and slowly let the breath go. "My beautiful daughter, you have always been a glass half-full sort of person. And I love that about you. But, not everything in life can be wrapped up and finished off with a pretty little bow."

Her mother was right; she had always believed that things would work out for her in the end. No, she hadn't expected to fall in love with a man from Australia, and she certainly hadn't planned on being pregnant in her twenties. Her dream, her post-graduate plan, had always been to build Sugar Creek's quarter horse breeding and training business. As far as her personal life was concerned, she had always wanted to meet the right man, marry, settle down and build a family on her stake on the family ranch. Even though he had come along sooner than she had planned, Hawk Bowhill *was* that true love she had imagined; Hawk was her present, her future and her forever.

Jessie rested her hands on her small baby bump. "I'm getting everything I've always dreamed of, Mama. I have my quarter horses and now I have Hawk and our baby."

After a moment, Lilly stood up to beckon her and Savannah over. First, Lilly kissed Savannah on her forehead, and then she kissed the forehead of her youngest child.

Holding their hands, Lilly said, "I am so happy that you are blessing our family with more children. I love you both. So much. May God continue to bless you with happy and healthy children."

"Thank you." Savannah had tears swimming in her emerald green eyes.

"Thank you, Mama." Jessie threw her arms around her mother's shoulders. "I'm so sorry I didn't tell you right from the start."

With her thumb, Lilly wiped a tear from Jessie's cheek. "Don't upset yourself with the past, little one."

"But Dad—"

"Let me handle your father," Lilly said evenly. "Okay?"

Jessie wanted to believe that Lilly could fix what she had just broken with Jock, but her father was as angry as a hungry bear coming out of a long winter of hibernation. Lilly was powerful, but perhaps even her power had limitations.

"Okay," Jessie agreed. At the same time she responded to her mother, she heard loud, strident footsteps approaching the dining room. Hawk strode into the dining room with a grim expression on his face.

Jessie went to his side immediately.

"What happened?" she asked, even though she had enough evidence to guess that it went *horribly*.

"Later." That one word spoke volumes, as did the

red undertone in his skin. He was furious—perhaps more angry than she'd ever seen him.

She nodded her agreement.

Hawk hugged her tightly, kissed her on the top of her head and then walked over to Lilly. He held out his hand to her. "I'm sorry we met under these circumstances, Mrs. Brand. It was never my intention to disrespect your husband or you."

Lilly ignored Hawk's extended hand and hugged him instead. This was the magic of her mother; Lilly was always working to sand down the rough edges that Jock's temper left behind. Always.

"Welcome to the family, Hawk," her mother said sweetly. "The road is a bit bumpy now, but it'll smooth out sooner or later."

"Yes, ma'am."

Hawk and Bruce shook hands, and Jessie hugged Savannah one last time before they headed to the foyer hand in hand. Hawk grabbed his Stetson off the hook and put it on. Behind them, she heard her father's office door open. She turned around to find her father staring at them, his face looking as if it had been chiseled out of granite.

She hesitated for the briefest of seconds before she said to Hawk, "Hold on one minute."

Hawk didn't try to interfere and she knew that he wouldn't. Hawk was a family-oriented gentleman— it was one of the many things she loved about him. He would never want to cause a rift between her and her family. After all, she was the one who had messed up the whole entire meeting, not him. Part of the reason she had kept her plan a secret was because Hawk wouldn't have gone along with it.

Jessie trotted over to her father, threw herself into his arms and hugged him tightly. She gave a kiss on the cheek and said, "I love him, Dad. I really do. And he loves me. You'll see. He really does."

Jock held on to her as if she would disappear into thin air. "I love you, baby girl."

She gave her father one last kiss on the cheek before she headed back to Hawk. It felt horrible to have her father so disappointed and angry with her; it felt even worse knowing that Jock didn't approve of Hawk, and of their marriage, no matter how irrational his feelings were. Hawk opened the front door for her to walk through. She saw Hawk give her father one last look and politely tip his hat to the elder man before he followed her out the door.

"I'm sorry, Hawk." She had her arm hooked tightly with his arm. "That was a disaster."

They reached her car without Hawk saying a word. He opened the driver's-side door for her, but she didn't get in. Instead, she turned toward him, put her hand on his chest and said with her face upturned, "Talk to me."

"He wouldn't give me his blessing to marry you."

Jessie felt like her heart was squeezed inside her chest. She swallowed several times, knowing that underneath his stoic expression he was hurting inside.

"What does that mean for us?" she asked.

He locked eyes with hers, and as it always was, it felt as if they were touching each other's souls whenever their eyes met and held.

"It means," he said in an even, calm tone, "that we have a lot of work to do with your father."

"But that would have been true no matter how he found out about the visa…and about our baby."

"You're probably right."

"I'm absolutely right." She kept her hands on his chest. "But what does that mean for us exactly? We have less than ninety days to get married."

"I know."

"What if my father doesn't approve before our time is up?" She heard the renewed anxiety in her voice.

Hawk took her hands in his; he kissed the back of each hand and then dropped a quick kiss on her lips. "Then we'll get married without his blessing."

Jessie freed her hands from his so she could wrap her arms around him. She rested her check on his chest. "Oh, thank goodness. I was worried that you were going to say that if he didn't approve, you wouldn't marry me."

"I was meant for you and you were meant for me." Hawk hugged her back reassuringly, his chin resting lightly on the top of her head. "No one, *nothing*, is going to keep us apart. Not an ocean, not a continent, not our families. You and me, we're a done deal."

Chapter Four

It had taken Jock Brand several shots of whiskey and a fine cigar smoked outside on his deck to calm down enough to go upstairs to bed. Lilly had sat quietly beside him, all the while refraining from reminding him of his doctor's orders. When he was finally ready to go to bed, Lilly started her nightly routine of checking all the downstairs locks and turning off the majority of lights while he took his shower.

"Don't be too long," Jock said to his wife when she came into the bedroom. He was propped up in their massive bed impatiently waiting for Lilly to join him. After so many years of marriage, Jock couldn't seem to fall asleep if his wife wasn't in bed with him.

"I won't." Lilly smiled at him as she headed into the master bathroom. The sound of her nightly routine—opening and closing of drawers, the sound of the faucet being turned on and off—gave him comfort. He could always count on his beloved Lilly.

Lilly turned off the bathroom light and came into the bedroom wearing a simple yellow silk sheath, her silver laced raven locks loose down her back. He reached over and pulled her side of the covers back. With a sweet, loving smile, she slipped into their bed and into his arms.

Jock pulled her close to him. "He's going to take her away from us."

"He's here to make a life with our daughter in Montana."

"He's going to take her away from us," he said. "Don't ask me how. I just know. I feel it in my gut."

"What's done is done, my love. They love each other. They have a baby on the way. But Jessie will always be *our* baby. She *can't* be taken away from us."

Jessie awakened while it was still dark the next morning with an unexpected bout of nausea. She had an easy first trimester and wondered, as she emerged from the bathroom, if her second trimester was going to be much worse. That was her thought as she made her way down the short hallway to the kitchen and living room. She expected to find Hawk on the couch or sitting in a chair watching the sunrise, but neither of those theories panned out.

She stopped and looked around. "Hawk?"

When she had awakened with morning sickness,

Hawk hadn't been in bed beside her. During their time together in Brisbane, Hawk always was the first one to open his eyes, but he would always linger in bed until she awoke. Wearing Hawk's oversize Brisbane Lions football jersey and with her feet bare, Jessie opened the front door of Liam's cabin in the hopes of locating her fiancé. On the porch railing she found a nearly full bottle of Jack Daniels whiskey and a small empty tumbler beside it. Sometime after she had finally managed to toss and turn her way to sleep, Hawk had gotten out of bed to have a nightcap.

"Hawk?" Jessie put the empty tumbler back in its place on the wooden railing.

She quickly went down the porch stairs and looked around the clearing. There, on a patch of green grass, was Hawk lying flat on the ground, dressed, hat covering his face and his booted feet crossed at the ankles.

"Hawk!" she called his name loudly as she stepped off the last stair of the porch onto the dewy ground.

Her foot hit a rock or two on her way over to her fiancé, which made her repeat "ouch" several times. The ground was damp and cold, two sensations she didn't enjoy.

"Hawk!" she said, annoyance creeping into her voice.

Hawk lifted his hat off his face and looked over at her through squinted, unfocused eyes. "What the devil? Why are you yelling?" He sat up and situated his hat back on his head. It was his old, worn-out Australian hat, not the Stetson she had bought for him.

The morning light was faint with a hint of glowing orange peeking over the mountain range in the distance. The air was so still that Jessie could easily hear the sounds of mooing cows being fed in a pasture on the other side of forest at the back half of Liam's property line.

Hands on her hips, and still feeling a little cruddy, Jessie frowned at him. "Why are you sleeping out here? Why aren't you sleeping in bed with me?"

Having gotten his bearings, Hawk stood up. "I'm used to sleeping outside in the bush."

"This isn't the bush, Hawk." She brushed the dirt and little pieces of grass from the back of his shirt.

"I know," he said, and he sounded homesick to her ears, "but falling asleep on the ground listening to the cows talking to each other made it feel more like home."

They stood together in silence before Jessie slipped her hand into his so they could walk back to the cabin together. Did it make her feel good that Hawk felt so homesick that he had to leave the bed to sleep on the hard ground? No, it sure didn't. But she couldn't fault him. Hawk had given up so much to be with her; whatever he needed to do to adjust to life in Montana, she intended to support him.

"I'll see if we can borrow a sleeping bag from one of my brothers. If you're going to make this a habit, at least you can be more comfortable."

"Naw." He grabbed the bottle of whiskey and empty glass on their way inside. "That'll make me soft."

Jessie reached out to squeeze his rock-hard bicep. "No one could accuse you of being soft, handsome."

Hawk smiled at her; he had such a great smile and such compelling, vibrant eyes. She imagined having many more children with his incredible smile and moss green eyes.

"Pickins are slim, my friend." She opened the fridge. "Cold cereal and coffee is the best I can do. We'll need to head into town to pick up some supplies. We cannot survive on love alone."

"Speak for yourself." He walked behind her to wrap her up in his strong arms. She squirmed playfully when he kissed the back of her neck.

"Care for a quickie?" Hawk held on to her as he nibbled her ear.

"*Quickie* is false advertising with you, sir." Smiling, she spun around in his arms. "I've got to get something in my stomach. I woke up feeling sick."

His expression shifted from playful to concerned. "Are you okay?"

She nodded, swallowing several times against the nausea. "Morning sickness."

Hawk frowned. "Then you sit down and I'll serve you. One decaf coffee and cold cereal coming right up."

Jessie sat down on a bar stool and rested her chin in her head. "Have I told you lately that I love you?"

"Not today," he said in a matter-of-fact manner.

"I love you."

He winked at her with a smile. "I love you too, gorgeous."

She smiled at him. "I have a lot planned for us today."

"What's on the agenda?"

"After breakfast, I'll take you to the foaling barn so you can see my office, meet my mares and my stallion."

"Sounds good."

"And then I'll take you to our stake on the ranch. A creek runs through it, and it has so many prime building spots—flat land for pastures. It's a little piece of heaven," she said. "How does that sound?"

"It sounds brilliant." Hawk set a bowl of bran cereal in front of her, poured milk over it and then handed her a spoon. "Our own slice of paradise, is it?"

She took a bite of cereal, chewed quickly and nodded. "It really is. I can see us raising children there and having our own herd of quarter horses. I've had my eye on a stallion in Wyoming for a while now. I can't even begin to tell you how much of my life I've spent fantasizing about building a house on that property and settling down with my husband. I didn't expect you to arrive so quickly!"

"So—" Hawk put on the coffee "—do you like the bloke who turned up for ya?"

Jessie smiled at him. "*You* are better than all of my fantasy husbands rolled into one."

"Now that's what I like to hear."

"Well, let's face it, handsome—" Jessie smiled

in spite of her lingering morning sickness "—the
accent and those biceps absolutely tipped the scales
in your favor."

On the way to the Jeep, Jessie tossed the keys to
Hawk. "We're only going to be driving on Sugar
Creek land. You may as well start getting used to
driving on the right side of the road."

"I'll take a crack at it." He caught the keys easily.
Once behind the wheel, Hawk cranked the engine
and shifted into gear. "I've been pretty keen to do
this. Let's see how we go."

They backtracked on the dirt road that took them
past Bruce and Savannah's house and used one of
the offshoot roads that skirted Gabe and Bonita's
Little Sugar Creek.

"It's not so bad." Hawk looked to be having fun
navigating the bumpy back roads that crisscrossed
the ranch. He picked up things easily, so Jessie never
doubted that he would master driving on the left side
of the car and the right side of the road after some
practice.

"A lot like driving in the bush," she mused, letting
her arm dangle out of the open window. They had
to travel for an hour on orange clay roads to reach
the main ranch house his grandfather had built on
Daintree Downs.

She took every opportunity to highlight parallel
examples between life in the Australian outback and
life on a Montana cattle ranch. She was acutely aware

of an underlying depression she sensed in Hawk, especially after seeing him asleep on the ground. If she hadn't gotten pregnant, would he be in Montana? No.

"Stop!" she exclaimed. Hawk slammed on the brakes. "Back up!"

Hawk did as he was instructed while Jessie looked toward Little Sugar Creek. "What the heck is going on there?"

Through the woods, Jessie saw bulldozers clearing a large area of land. Something odd was happening on Gabe's property.

"Take a right here and just follow the road all the way to where those bulldozers are. I need to check this out."

As the Jeep approached the construction zone, Jessie spotted her brother Gabe and his wife, Bonita, standing nearby watching the workers clear their land.

"That's Gabe!" She pointed to her brother. "He's home!"

Hawk parked away from the work of the heavy equipment. The moment it was safe, Jessie opened the door, slammed it shut behind her and raced over to where her brother was standing.

"Gabe!" she called out. "Bonnie!"

Her brother turned toward her voice, and his face lit up when he caught sight of her, as did his wife's. Jessie had a strong bond with all of her siblings, but her relationship with Gabe had been extra special. Ever since he was a boy, Gabe had connected on a soul level with horses—with kindness and patience, he could get horses to do anything he asked of them. As an adult, Gabe had dedicated his life to horses, as a trainer, long-distance hauler and overall horse whisperer.

"There she is!" Gabe opened his arms to absorb the force of her flying into him.

More so than any of the brothers, Gabe resembled Jock, pulling from his Scottish heritage, with a more ruddy skin tone, compact frame, dusty brown hair and, of course, those striking Brand blue eyes. Even though Gabe wasn't the tallest of the brothers, he was strong as an ox and could arm-wrestle just about any man and win.

Her brother swung her around several times before putting her feet down on the ground. The second her feet touched, she greeted Bonnie, careful not to squish the couple's geriatric, three-legged rescue Chihuahua, Tater. Dr. Bonita Delafuente-Brand, a family physician, was a beautiful woman with dark, brown eyes, a slender willowy build and thick long black hair. Bonita's heritage held deep roots in Mexico. Gabe's lifelong love affair with horses had led him to the love of his life when he was hired by Bonita's father to haul her dressage horse from Virginia to Montana. On that trip, Gabe and Bonita had fallen in love.

"Don't go anywhere!" Jessie told them.

"We're not," Gabe said.

"I want you to meet Hawk!"

Jessie spun around on her heel and booked it back to Hawk, who was now walking toward her.

"Sorry," she said a bit breathlessly as she reached for his hand.

"No worries," Hawk said. "You love your family and I love that about you."

Jessie beamed up at him, proud to be on his arm. When they reached her brother and sister-in-law, Hawk offered Gabe his hand and looked him straight in the eye.

"I'm Hawk," her fiancé said.

"Gabe," her brother said. "And this is my wife, Bonnie."

"A pleasure." Hawk lifted his hat off his head to show Bonita respect.

"We're very happy to meet you," Bonnie said kindly. "We've heard so much about you."

"And this is Tater." Jessie petted the top of the tiny dog's head.

"Hello, mate." Hawk held out his finger for the dog to sniff. After a moment of very serious sniffing, Tater gave Hawk's outstretched finger one decisive lick.

"Well, that's a good sign." Bonnie laughed. "Tater has very discerning taste."

"To hear it from Pops, we were expecting you to have horns, a pitchfork and a tail." Gabe chuckled.

Hawk took the good-natured ribbing from her brother in stride. With a smile, he said, "We didn't make a brilliant first impression, I grant you that."

"But we did hear that congratulations are in order." Bonnie smiled knowingly.

Jessie leaned her body into Hawk's frame, her hands naturally going to her small baby bump.

"Thank you," she said to her sister-in-law. "We're both super excited."

Gabe angled a disapproving look at Hawk before he said to her, "I thought you were going to wait until you were thirty to go down that road."

Jessie would normally wither under that kind of inspection from Gabe; this time she didn't. Confidently, she said, "Well, the road came a bit quicker than I thought."

Bonnie, as was her way, worked to diffuse the tension that had just cropped up between them. "Life happens. I thought I would be practicing medicine in a big city hospital."

"But Gabe happened," Jessie said.

Bonnie turned loving eyes toward her husband. "He certainly did. And I fell in love with Montana. I never expected to embrace country life, but here I am."

Jessie smiled when she saw Gabe duck his head a bit and a blush creep up his neck. Her brother and his wife still acted like newlyweds. She hoped she would always be in love with Hawk, no matter what life threw their way.

"Speaking of things going on—" Jessie took the opportunity to change the subject away from her surprise pregnancy "—what's going on here?"

Her sister-in-law's face lit up with renewed excitement. "We are breaking ground to finally build our dream home."

Prior to her starting her own practice in Bozeman, Bonita had spent her formative years competing in dressage. Jessie knew how much her sister-in-law wanted an indoor riding arena so she could ride and train her horses—rain, shine or snow.

"The new barn and arena will be built right over there." Bonnie pointed.

Jessie was imagining the new house, barn and arena when something caught her attention. She looked over at the paddock behind the small barn Gabe had built on his property over a decade ago.

"Hey! Who's that?"

A stocky buckskin gelding hung its head over the fence. His body was a striking gold that offset his black mane and tail.

"That's Isabella's new barrel racer."

"Are you serious?" Jessie asked, happily surprised to hear that her brother Noah's daughter had taken up a sport she herself was passionate about. Noah was a was a major in the marines who manned the recruiting office in Bozeman. Even though Noah and his wife, Shayna, hadn't been at the brunch, they had both been supportive of her relationship with Hawk from the start.

Gabe nodded. "I picked him up on my way back. Noah bought her a great little trail pony for Christmas, but she needed a horse that could get her started in barrel racing."

"She's that good?" Jessie asked.

"She's a natural. Fearless, intuitive. So much like you when you first started, it's pretty uncanny," Gabe said of his young niece.

"I'll have to show her some of my tricks," Jessie said, partly wishing she hadn't given up the sport during her college years.

"I think you should."

After a few more minutes catching up and taking a moment to welcome the new gelding to Sugar Creek, Jessie and Hawk headed back to the Jeep so she could show him the foaling barn and introduce him to her herd of quarter horses before heading to the land where they would build their home.

Jessie pulled up to the large foaling barn that had been her focus for the last year. Together, they walked into the ten-stall barn with a wide aisle.

"Here's my office." She opened the door to her office, where she had spent most of her time during their yearlong courtship. Focusing on her beloved horses had made her longing for Hawk more bearable.

After Jessie showed him her breeding logs and all of the orders for stallion semen and waiting lists for horses she had personally trained, she walked him through the barn that she had transformed.

"Everything here has been redone," she said, stopping at a stall to pet a pretty roan mare. "Foaling mats have been put in the stalls, I added windows and fans to optimize ventilation."

"I wish I had this kind of set-up at Daintree Downs," Hawk said, noticeably impressed.

Jessie linked her arm with his, happy to finally be sharing her lifelong passion with him. She walked him to the end of the barn and led him to a grassy, fenced-in pasture.

At the gate, Jessie put her fingers up to her lips and sounded a loud, long whistle. Shadow, her most prized quarter horse, lifted his head, snorted several times, before he galloped full-tilt toward them.

"This is Shadow."

With a laugh, she climbed up onto a fence rail and greeted the handsome blue roan stallion with a hug.

"Isn't he incredible?" Jessie scratched the stallion's ears, one of the horse's favorite spots to be scratched.

"He's a real looker."

"And he's so strong." Jessie climbed down off the fence. "He's got the best confirmation of any quarter horse we've ever had here. Do you remember seeing all of those trophies in my office?"

Hawk nodded, reaching out to pet the stallion's heavily muscled neck.

"All for Shadow," she bragged proudly. "All for my fella."

"Hey!" Hawk teased her. "I thought that *I* was your fella!"

Jessie wrapped her arm around him and hugged him tightly. "You will always be my fella."

"But?" Hawk asked her.

"*But*, Shadow will always be my *four-legged* fella." She looked up into her fiancé's face. "Can you live with that?"

He took the opportunity to kiss her. "I can live with it."

After Jessie showed Hawk the foaling barn and introduced him to Shadow, her mares and their foals, Jessie drove on the narrow road that led to Oak Tree Hill, her brother Hunter's stake, which was rough, rocky and overgrown. Jessie and Hawk came to a fork in the road; Hunter's land was on the left, while hers abutted his.

"Do you see that boulder?" She pointed to a giant stone laced with granite and other minerals native to Montana. "That's where our land starts."

After the fork in the road, and once they drove onto her property, all that was left was raw land. They drove a ways into the tall grass in what could be a perfect spot for cattle or a herd of horses to graze. Hawk parked the Jeep and they both jumped out.

Hawk tipped his hat back on his head, his hands on his hips, as he took in the land before him.

"Our land goes all the way back to that smaller mountain over there." Jessie pointed. "We could fence in this area right in front of us."

"Good grazing." Hawk nodded. Her fiancé seemed to be mapping out the land before him, and that gave Jessie hope for his future happiness at Sugar Creek.

Arm in arm, they forged a path through the thigh-high grass to the woods. Jessie wanted to show Hawk her favorite part of her stake—the creek that had drawn her to this part of the ranch even when she was a kid exploring on her horse.

"This is gorgeous," he said as they approached the water.

"I knew you would love this as much as I do."

"Absolutely, I do." He put his arm around her shoulders.

Her stomach flip-flopped in a lovely way. She wanted Hawk to feel at home on the ranch as soon as possible. His life on the cattle station was wild and wide open. Their hundred-acre stake on Sugar Creek would feel like he was living on a postage stamp in contrast to his million-acre station. But it was beautiful, secluded and peaceful here. That part Jessie had been certain would appeal to Hawk.

Hawk took off his hat, knelt down by the stream and washed the sweat off his face and neck. They sat down on the bank of the stream side by side, arm in arm. Hawk gave her a sweet kiss during a long stretch of silence, and she leaned her head on his shoulder. It was the best feeling to have the man she loved sitting by the creek with her. It was a dream come true.

"How are you feeling?" Hawk asked her, his concerned eyes on her face. "How's our little one?"

"Better." She nodded. "I'm actually starting to get hungry. How about you?"

"Famished," he said. "Yeah. I could go for a bite to eat."

"Why don't we head into town, grab some lunch and pick up some groceries?"

"Sounds like a winner." Hawk stood up and offered her his hand.

Fingers entwined, they retraced their steps through the open field toward the Jeep. Jessie got behind the wheel, cranked the engine, turned around and headed back toward Little Sugar Creek, where she could easily cut through to the main road.

"We're heading into town." Jessie stopped the Jeep where her brother and his wife were standing. "Do you need anything?"

"We're good," Gabe said. "Thank you!"

As Jessie pulled out onto the main road, she glanced over at Hawk. He seemed to have drifted into a pensive place.

"I'm glad that you got to meet Gabe and Bonnie."

"Me too."

She glanced over at him again, worried.

"Did you like him?"

He gave her a quick smile. "Yeah, sure. He seems like a good bloke."

After some silence between them, Jessie said, "It's a lot, I know. New country, new life, a baby, a wife…"

"Seven brothers."

"Seven brothers," she agreed with a small laugh. "I know you just got here. I know that. And of course, it hasn't been easy with my dad. But now that you've seen the ranch and met some of my family, do you think that you can be happy here?"

Hawk knew how Jessie wanted him to feel about her beloved Sugar Creek. Of course, he could see the beauty of Sugar Creek, Montana, and how much his fiancée loved the family cattle spread. But it wasn't Daintree Downs. And just like Sugar Creek was for Jessie—a family legacy—so too was Daintree Downs to him. The major difference being that the land holdings that made up the cattle station he stood to inherit had been in his family for four generations. Love for that land was, quite literally, embedded in his DNA.

"I'm happy to be with you," he said truthfully. "I'm happy to be marrying you and starting a family with you."

He saw Jessie tighten her fingers on the steering wheel; he knew what she wanted him to say, but he just couldn't.

"You already know that I wanted you to fall in love with my farm and my way of life. I had hoped that after meeting our little community in Cunnamulla that you could see yourself there. But this is where we are, and I'm going to give it a go."

Hawk had been down this road many times before with women. They liked the idea of an outback cowboy and the trappings that came with a cattle baron's success. But when they came to the point of them leaving everything and everyone behind to live a secluded hard life in the outback, the women headed back to civilization. One big difference now: Jessie was, in his mind, his true soulmate, and she was pregnant with his child. The only thing that mattered to him more than continuing the family legacy at Daintree Downs was being there for the mother of his child. But there was no getting around the fact that the sacrifice was enormous. The pain of leaving everything he had ever known behind and devastating his grandfather was real. He couldn't deny that.

"But if I wasn't pregnant, you wouldn't be here," Jessie said, her eyes focused on the road ahead.

Before he could answer, the phone rang and interrupted the conversation.

"It's Mom," she said, and Hawk nodded as she picked up the call. Jessie listened to her mother and then finally said, "Okay. We're going to grab lunch and get some groceries. We'll be over after."

Jessie hung up the phone. "Mom and Dad want to meet with us when we get back to the ranch."

Hawk didn't have high hopes for his relationship with his future father-in-law. And he had been damn well offended when Jock accused him of wanting to marry his daughter for a zard. But if sitting down with Jock again was the price of admission to the Brand family, he was more than willing to pay. Even though he was perfectly willing to marry Jessie without Jock's blessing, he was old-fashioned enough to want her father's stamp of approval.

"Are you ready for that?" his love asked, concerned.

"I'm ready," Hawk said. Facing Jock was no different than wrangling a scrub bull out in the bush. Scrub bulls were bulls that had gone wild, and they were notoriously dangerous, foul-tempered and nearly impossible to catch. But as all of Hawk's friends back home knew, he was one of the best scrub bull wranglers in Queensland.

"I'd rather do it straightaway," he told Jessie. He couldn't imagine sitting through a meal knowing the conversation that was looming on their horizon.

"You mean right now?" she asked, surprised.

"Yeah." His life in the Australian outback had taught him to stand his ground and to never back down from a fight. "Right now."

Chapter Five

"It'll be fine," Jessie said as she hooked her arm with Hawk's after they entered the foyer of her father and mother's palatial log cabin mansion.

"It'll work itself out eventually," her fiancé agreed.

"Don't be nervous," she instructed, but in reality, she seemed much more nervous than Hawk. As usual, he had an inscrutable expression on his handsome face, and there was steeliness in his mossy green eyes.

"I don't feel nervous."

Jessie glanced up at him. "Then don't get mad."

"I won't."

"Or combative."

Hawk stopped walking so he could look her in the eyes. "I've got this, Jess."

She wanted to remind him of the last time he met

with Jock but batted the words away as soon as they formed in her brain. Hawk was an even-tempered man, for the most part, but he could blow his top if the right buttons were pushed. And one thing her father was good at *was* finding people's buttons and pushing them for sport.

"Okay," she said after a couple of seconds ticked by. "I'm just nervous."

He brought her hand up to kiss it as he often did. This made her smile; even at their most tense times, Hawk was always ready to show her, in words and deeds, just how much he loved her. So it was with that bolstering of her love that put the wind in her sails as she entered her father's office arm in arm with the man who would be the father of her children and her lover for a lifetime.

When they entered Jock's office, her father was sitting in his executive chair turned toward the expansive view of cows grazing in the far distance; his back was facing the door.

Jessie gave Hawk's arm a quick pat before she went to go greet her father.

"Hi, Dad."

Jock spun his chair around at the sound of her voice, his face alight with love for her, his youngest child. But it didn't take a body language expert to see the scowl that crossed his face when he caught sight of Hawk.

Jessie leaned down, hugged her father tightly and

kissed him on the cheek, which was their typical greeting.

"Hello, sir." Hawk had followed her over to where her father sat.

Even though Jock didn't respond to his polite greeting, Hawk extended his hand for her father to shake. Jock, stubborn as always, refused to shake her fiancé's hand.

"Daddy." Jessie frowned at him disappointedly. "At least shake his hand."

Jock grumbled something under his breath but gave Hawk's hand one strong shake before he withdrew his hand as if the younger man's skin had burned him.

The ruddy undertone to Jock's skin began to deepen, signaling to Jessie that her father was already getting riled up at the sight of Hawk, and they hadn't even begun to get into the main course of their discussion.

"Where's Mama?"

"She's either in her greenhouse or her sewing room," Jock said stiffly. Jessie had hoped that the morning would bring a brighter outlook on the current situation for her father. Those hopes, however naive, were dashed quickly by her father's attitude. He looked as if he would like to hog-tie Hawk and throw him on a barge bound for Australia. Not one bit of softening happened overnight.

"Well, I just texted and she hasn't gotten back," Jessie said as she dialed her mother's number.

Simultaneous to her call, a phone on Jock's desk began to ring. Jessie started to shift piles of paper around until she unearthed her mother's phone.

"Well, that's why Mom hasn't answered her phone." Jessie hit the red End button on her phone screen. "I'm going to have to go find her."

"Okay," Hawk said.

"Fine." That was her father's one-word response.

Jessie hesitated to leave the two of them alone together; she absolutely believed that her two most important men could derail the conversation with lightning speed, and all would be said and done before she could return with Lilly, the family's most successful arbiter.

"Dad—" she leveled a look at him "—please be nice."

Jock's eyes snapped at her in annoyance, but she counted it as a win that he didn't protest verbally.

"Hawk," she addressed her fiancé, "please sit down. You're making me nervous just standing there."

Her second win of the day was when Hawk took a seat in a chair opposite Jock's desk.

"I'll be right back."

"Make it quick," Jock grumbled. "I'm hungry."

"That makes two of us," Hawk said.

"Well," Jessie said with a chipper smile that was sure to annoy her father and her fiancé, "see that? And the two of you thought you didn't have anything in common."

Simultaneously, Jock and Hawk said, "Jessie."

On her way out of the office, Jessie had a broad smile on her face because it just occurred to her that her father and fiancé were more alike than she had originally imagined. Yes, Jock's anger boiled over quickly while Hawk's was a slow burn. But they were both strong masculine men who often found themselves thwarted or circumvented by the equally strong women they loved. For all of his bluster, her father had never tried to clip her wings. He usually didn't like it, but he always let her fly in whatever direction her dreams took her. And since she had flown straight into the arms of an Australian cowboy, sooner or later, Jock would find a way to be okay with that reality. It was this positive thought that propelled Jessie up the grand, winding staircase to the second floor to her mother's sewing and craft room.

"Why don't we sit over here where we can all be comfortable?" Lilly said after she gave Jock a hug.

Hawk had been gazing at the large antique grandfather clock standing at attention between two floor-to-ceiling bookcases. The ticking of the clock was the only sound in the room, with the exception of the occasional throat clearing and barely audible grumbling coming from the other side of the desk. Hawk had tried to strike up a conversation with Jock, but the man refused to answer, staring right through him.

Jessie held out her hand for him, and he was happy to take it. Anything that moved this situation along was good for him. He knew that he would have a tough row to hoe with Jessie's parents and, perhaps, even some of her seven siblings. On the other hand, having Jock wanting to send him packing back to Australia hadn't been one of the options on his mind.

Jock's office was large enough to house a long leather couch, a coffee table and two large chairs with overstuffed armrests and cushions across the way. He sat down next to Jess on the couch while Jock and Lilly settled into the chairs.

"I'd like to start," Jess said, holding on to his hand, her shoulder and thigh pressed securely into his body.

"Please." Lilly nodded.

"I am truly sorry that I made a mess of this whole situation. I suppose I was worried about how the both of you would react to me rushing into marriage with a man you hadn't even met before."

Jock looked at his wife. "You told me that he was the rebound guy."

"I said *probably*. Probably the rebound guy."

"Well, he bounced right onto my land, right into my house!"

"Jock," Lilly said in a cajoling manner, "we're here to figure things out."

"How can we figure things out when none of this makes a bit of sense? Our daughter is pregnant, and now she's rushing into a marriage…" Jock stood up and began to pace in front of the nearby hearth.

"Again," Jessie reiterated, "I understand that all of this is a bit of a shock."

"Yes, it was a shock," Lilly agreed, "but, now it's time to move past that."

Jock grumbled something under his breath while he continued to pace.

"And I do see now that I didn't handle it correctly." Jessie glanced over at him with a sincerely regretful expression on her pretty oval face. "I just want you both to know that Hawk had no idea that I had kept all of this a secret. He handled his family and I handled mine."

"Please sit down, Jock," Lilly said, her hands folded on her lap. "You know the pacing gives me a headache."

"Yes, dear," he said, and then rejoined the group.

"You didn't handle this correctly, I think we can all agree to that," Lilly said.

"Yes," Jock, Jessie and he all said in unison.

"What's done is done," her mother said pragmatically. "We now need to find a path forward as a family."

At the word *family*, Jock's lips turned down severely, and he crossed his arms in front of his body, then rested his hands on his rounded belly.

Lilly appeared keenly aware of her husband's body language and ignored it as she continued.

"How long do you have until you need to be married?" the elder woman asked.

"Eighty-five days now," Jessie said.

"Too damn soon," Jock snapped.

"It is quick," Lilly agreed in a gentler manner.

"You do realize, daughter, that our entire family is prepping for Callie's wedding."

Jessie nodded. "I know. It's bad timing."

Jock harrumphed at that. "*Horrible* timing."

"Callie's wedding has to take precedence," Lilly said.

"Of course." Jessie nodded. "Hawk and I have already discussed this, and we would be happy to get married at the courthouse and then plan a formal wedding later."

"Or perhaps we could throw something together for Callie's rehearsal dinner. We're holding it here, and for the first time in years, the entire family will be together." Jessie's mom sat back in her chair, seeming more relaxed. "Of course, you'd have to get approval from Kate and Callie."

Jessie turned to him. "What do you think?"

"As long as I get to marry you, just tell me where and when, and I'll be there."

His fiancée hugged him affectionately beneath the sour gaze of her father.

"What do you think, Jock?" Lilly turned to her husband.

"What do I think?" he asked.

Lilly nodded.

"What do I think?" Jock repeated the question again.

No one spoke while they waited for him to continue.

"I think," Jessie's father said, "that this all stinks

to high heaven, like a fresh pile of cow manure, that's what I think. I'm having a wedding crammed down my throat, and I don't know one damn thing about you other than the fact that you got my daughter pregnant without the sanctity of marriage. That's what I think!"

"Mr. Brand, I know none of this is sitting well with you and I hope in time we will be able to start over with each other," Hawk said in plain language. "For now, I would like to ask for your daughter's hand in marriage. I would like your blessing to marry Jessie."

"Different day, same answer," Jock said. "Hell no. I won't give you my blessing."

Lilly frowned at her husband. "Stubborn man."

Jessie's mother stood up, rounded the coffee table and then held out her hands to both of them. Hawk stood up and so too did Jessie.

Holding both of their hands, Jessie's mother said, "We do give you our blessing."

"No, we don't," Jock interjected.

"And we are so happy to welcome a new grandchild into our family," Lilly continued.

"Thank you, Mama." Jessie hugged Lilly tightly.

"Thank you, Mrs. Brand," Hawk said sincerely. Hawk could see how important it was to have Lilly on their side.

"Call me Mom or Lilly. Take your pick. Family doesn't stand on formality."

"Thank you, Lilly," Hawk said, feeling a connection with Jessie's mother for the first time.

"Well, if we're done here, I've got bills to pay," Jock grumbled as he headed back to his desk.

"Jock," Lilly said in a loving yet slightly admonishing tone, "please come over and shake this young man's hand. He is to be our only son-in-law and the father of our grandchild."

Jock paused, his shoulders tense, before he fulfilled his wife's request. Jock stuck out his hand and Hawk accepted it.

Jock caught his eye and then he said, "You've got a lot to prove here."

"Yes, sir."

Jessie's father pulled his hand back and headed to the safety and comfort of his desk.

In a lowered voice, Lilly did her best to reassure them, "Just give him some time. He'll come around. You'll see."

"That was intense," Jessie said once they reached the foyer of the main house.

Hawk nodded wordlessly. She had never seen her fiancé rattled, not even when he was doing something incredibly dangerous, like catching wild bulls on Daintree Downs. In fact, when faced with danger, Hawk typically became calmer and more focused. But not after dealing with her parents.

"Now I really am starving," she said, her stomach feeling hollow from missing lunch. "How about you?"

Her phone ringing interrupted his response.

"Hi, dork," she said to her brother Bruce.

"Hi, brat," Bruce tossed back affectionately. "Where's Hawk?"

"He's right here. Why?"

"I've been trying to call him," her brother said.

"Did you turn your phone off?" she asked Hawk. "Bruce has been trying to call."

"Yeah." Her fiancé opened the front door, and they both walked through.

"He didn't have the phone on. We just finished with Dad and Mama."

"Well, then, my timing is probably perfect. Ask Hawk if he wants to go move some cattle with me."

"Did you hear that?" she asked Hawk.

Hawk nodded. "I could do with a bit of mustering."

"He said yes."

"I'll pick him up at my house in ten."

Jessie hung up the phone and then tossed Hawk the keys to her Jeep. "Are you sure you want to move cattle on an empty stomach?"

"I'm not hungry." Hawk cranked the engine.

That was a first. Hawk was, at least from her experience, always ready to eat.

"Hey…" she said, staring at his profile.

"Hey, yourself, gorgeous," Hawk said to her with a wink, but the tension in his jaw, neck and forehead didn't change.

"I love you."

"I love you too," he said, pulling onto the back road that would lead them to Bruce and Savannah's house.

"You must love me to put up with my dad," she said with a self-conscious laugh. "That was objectively horrible."

Hawk put on the brakes, stopped the Jeep and then leaned over for a kiss. And then she felt it again, that same spark that always ignited when their lips touched. Still holding her chin in place with his fingers, Hawk said as he looked deeply into her eyes, "You are everything to me, Jess. My life doesn't work anymore without you in it. So, whatever I have to do to fit in with your family, whatever I have to do to forge a relationship with your dad, I promise you, I'm gonna bloody well do it."

"Aunt Jessie!"

The moment her nieces Amanda and Isabella spotted her Jeep, they leapt off their swings and, along with a pack of seven rescue dogs, they ran toward her with wild abandon.

Jessie knelt down so she could absorb her nieces into her arms. The girls, both in first grade, had slender, lanky builds, and with the exception of their hair color, the two cousins could pass for twins.

"Did you come to play with us?" Amanda asked excitedly.

"Not today." She hugged each of the girls tightly.

"Why not?" Amanda pouted sincerely.

"I have to go see Aunt Kate and Cousin Callie."

"Can we go with you?" Isabella asked. Noah's daughter had her dark brown wavy hair in long pigtails.

"Not today," she said, joining Hawk in greeting the dogs.

"Aww!" Isabella also pouted her displeasure.

"Who's he?" Amanda had moved on from her disappointment and now had her attention trained on Hawk.

"This is Uncle Hawk."

"Uncle Hawk?" the two girls almost said in stereo, squinting against the sun as they studied her fiancé.

"You aren't married," Isabella pointed out.

"Not yet." Jessie leaned down, wrapped her arms around the girl's shoulders and tickled her for a few seconds. "But soon."

Isabella twirled out her arms, giggling. Hawk was sweet to each of her nieces, and he was just as sweet with all of Bruce and Savannah's rescue dogs.

Savannah, who had been working in her garden, walked toward them in a flowery, threadbare dress that had seen better days and a floppy straw hat to protect her fair, freckly skin from the sun.

"Bruce told me you were heading our way," Savannah said.

Savannah hugged them both, her face alight with happiness. Jessie had to believe that the glow in her sister-in-law's face and the sparkle in her beautiful green eyes were directly linked to the baby she was going to have with Bruce.

"I feel like the pack is growing." Jessie gave each dog some affection.

Savannah laughed. "It is growing."

Her sister-in-law pointed to one dog. "This is Patch." And then to another dog. "And this is Diego."

Savannah flashed a bright smile. "Hello, Hawk. It's good to see you again. Welcome to our home." Savannah gave Hawk a friendly, sisterly hug.

"Thank you. It's good to see you too."

As a group, they walked toward Savannah and Bruce's ranch-style house. "I heard you met with Lilly and Jock."

"Yes, we did." Jessie reached out for Hawk's hand as they walked slowly toward the house followed by the pack of dogs and the two young girls.

"And?" Savannah asked.

"Let's just say it's a work in progress," Jessie answered. "Dad can be so stubborn."

"A family trait," Savannah pointed out kindly.

Jessie couldn't deny that. She'd been accused of being stubborn once or twice.

Jessie and Hawk sat down on the porch swing while Savannah had the girls help her bring some iced tea out to them. The iced tea was sweetened with clover honey that Savannah collected from her beehives.

"It makes sense to have a ceremony at the big

house." Savannah sat down on the top step of the porch, holding her own glass of iced tea.

"I think so," Jessie agreed. "I'm going to head over to Kate and Liam's place to run the idea by Callie."

Savannah nodded, then asked Hawk, "How do you like Montana so far?"

"It's taking some getting used to, that's the short answer," Hawk said. "But there's no denying it's a beautiful place."

"I'm going to take Hawk on a bit of a prenuptials trip."

"A trip away might be a good idea. Let things cool off," her sister-in-law said. "Where are you going?"

"Yellowstone, Great Falls, and Lewis and Clark Caverns," she said. "There's so much to do here, it was difficult to narrow down."

"She wants to convince me to love it here." Hawk put his arm around her shoulders. He caught her eye. "But all that really matters is that I love *you*."

Chapter Six

Mustering a herd of cattle made Hawk feel alive and at home. The Western saddle felt different than his saddle in Australia, but he barely noticed the difference once he started to help Bruce push the herd to another pasture where the grass was more abundant for grazing.

Once the herd was moved, they found a shady spot to rest the horses and watch the herd. This was the first time Hawk had a moment with Bruce and he imagined that Jessie's oldest brother would have a few pointed questions for him.

"So," Bruce said after a bit, "Jessie."

"I know, mate," Hawk said, knowing exactly what Bruce was getting at without directly saying it. Bruce had asked him, as a friend, to take care of his sister in

Brisbane, and now she was pregnant with his child. "I didn't set out to fall in love with her. But the minute I saw her, I felt that immediate spark between us. Love at first sight for me and I think for her too."

Bruce didn't say anything, so Hawk continued, "She's gorgeous, she's funny and she's incredibly sweet. I love the fact that she's cheeky and willing to give anything a crack. She can muster cattle and handle a horse better than most of the blokes or *sheilas* in the outback. We muck about like best mates, I love that about her," Hawk said simply. "I want to spend the rest of my life with Jess. Get married, have a family, make her happy. I wouldn't have risked everything to be here if I wasn't one hundred percent committed."

"What do you mean that you've risked everything?"

Hawk shifted in the saddle to get more comfortable but had a feeling that the discomfort was coming from inside his body, not outside.

"Jess doesn't know this, mate. And I don't want her to know. She doesn't need to be worrying about me while she's pregnant."

"She won't hear it from me."

"My grandfather has threatened to change his will—cut me out completely."

Bruce moved his horse in a semicircle so he could be face-to-face with him. "Are you serious?"

"Yeah," Hawk answered. "If I don't go back to Australia within one week of his death and stay for five years, all of Daintree Down's assets, including the land and cattle, will be donated to the Australian government."

Bruce was stunned, and it showed readily on his face. "Your grandfather doesn't approve of Jessie?"

"He loves Jess," Hawk said. "That's not the problem."

"But he doesn't want you to live in Montana."

"No."

"Do you really think he'll do that? Disinherit you?"

Hawk had asked himself that same questions hundreds of times: Did he really think that his grandfather was capable of doing such a catastrophic thing? Perhaps he was in denial, but Hawk had to believe that his grandfather wouldn't, *couldn't*, go through with that threat.

"No," Hawk finally said, "I don't. I think he'll threaten it but I can't believe he'd really go through with it."

The land that was Daintree Downs had been farmed by four generations of Bowhill men. His grandfather, William Bowhill, only had one child— Hawk's father, William Bowhill Jr. His mother and father had died in an automobile accident when he was just a boy, which had made Hawk the only heir of William Sr. With the trend of large Australian cattle stations being bought by foreign governments or foreign private investors, William had, for years, worried about Daintree Downs suffering the same fate. It was inconceivable that his grandfather would ever let their land go to anyone other than the one person who could continue the Bowhill line.

"You've got to tell Jessie," Bruce said emphatically. "She wouldn't want you to give up your birthright."

"She didn't take to the outback. She tried to imagine herself there, but it just wasn't for her." Hawk continued, "And I can't really say that I blame her. Not everyone is built to live in the bush. Most people aren't. I was in a long-term relationship with a really nice girl, but she couldn't handle living so far away from her family and friends—with twelve hundred people, on a good day. And she was an Australian girl, not an American girl like Jess. We broke up and she married a guy from Sydney. I think she's got a couple of kids now. It's a big deal to ask someone to leave their country, family and friends and move to a place that's remote and isolated."

"But it's not like Jessie is a city girl. She grew up here on this ranch. She started riding before she could walk, and she's been moving cattle since grade school."

"I know, and I love it." Hawk rested his hands on the saddle horn. "But it can be a really tough life at the station, way tougher than this. Jess wasn't happy at Daintree during a short visit, that's the truth of it. It was all fun and games for a couple of weeks, sure, but we've been in drought for a while, so it's hot and dusty, the land is flat and it's not as pretty as this, if I'm being honest. It's kilometers away from civilization. She missed her family, she missed her friends, and she couldn't imagine raising our child there. I was really devastated, but what can I do? If Jessie's not happy, I'm not happy, that's the bottom line for me."

Bruce studied him silently for a second or two. "You really do love her."

"Of course I do. I never thought I would leave Daintree Downs for anyone or anything. It's been my mistress, my first true love," Hawk said, staring off into the distance. "I can live without the farm. I'll miss it, I'll mourn it, but I *can* live without it. But what kind of life would I have without Jess and our child? From where I sit, I believe it would be a bloody sad one."

"I can't say that I blame you there. My life without Savannah would be no life at all."

After the conversation had lulled for a bit, Bruce said, "Just two guys sitting on horses sharing our feelings. That's not awkward or weird."

Hawk laughed, his mood lightened. He wasn't used to "sharing" his feelings with another bloke either. "Sounds like the makings of a podcast. Two guys on horses sharing our feelings."

"No comment." Bruce shook his head. "Let's get back to safer territory. Are you hungry?"

"Starving. Instead of eating lunch, we met with your folks."

"That was your first mistake, brother, and losing this race is about to be your second," Bruce said, asking his horse to take off at a gallop. "The last one to the truck has to buy the winner a beer!"

Glad for the distraction, Hawk whipped his horse around, leaned forward and gave the horse his head so he could gallop full tilt. Bruce and he were neck and neck across the wild field. They whooped and hollered and raced all the way back to the truck.

Winded and laughing, Hawk said, "I won that hand's down. You owe me a coldie, mate."

Bruce swung out of his saddle onto the ground. "I gave you the fastest horse. Next time, you'll be buying the beer."

Hawk dismounted and led his horse to the back of the trailer. "I'm up for a rematch when Jess and I get back from our trip. Being back in the saddle and working with the herd cleared my head."

"If you want to work, I've got plenty."

"I'm keen to work." Hawk climbed into the passenger side of Bruce's work truck. "Once I get back, put me to work straightaway."

Bruce shifted into gear and headed them back to his homestead. "You got it, brother."

Jessie pulled onto the long gravel drive that would take her to the center of ranch that Liam shared with his wife, Kate. Kate was a master horsewoman who had designed techniques for developing a bond with horses and riding using bitless bridles that had made her a celebrity in the western part of the country. After inheriting the ranch from her father, she had built a large barn with an indoor riding arena, a facility that was used regularly for her ongoing clinics. People always felt comfortable being with their horses at Kate's clinic, and her business was booming.

Jessie parked in front of the barn sandwiched in between two four-door long-bed GMC trucks and hopped out. Liam and Kate had built their dream home on a tall bluff that overlooked the central part of the ranch. Liam and Kate's house was surprisingly modern in style, making use of tall windows on every floor to make the most of their spectacular view. Happily situated a short distance from the stable, round pen and paddocks sat a 1970s brick rancher; this was the house where Kate had lived when she was a child. And it was the house where she'd raised her daughter, Calico, as a single mother. Calico, a young adult living with Down syndrome, was known to her friends and family as Callie. Now, it served as wedding central but eventually it would be the home that Callie shared with her husband-to-be, Tony Jr.

Jessie knocked on the front door of the older brick ranch; according to Liam, this was the center of all things wedding, and she was pretty certain she would catch Callie and Kate there.

"Aunt Jessie!" Callie opened the door for her.

"Hi, Callie." Jessie hugged her niece.

When Liam fell in love with Kate, he knew that Callie was part of the deal. And even though Callie was already a young adult when he married her mother, Liam formally adopted her. The entire Brand family loved Callie and had taken her into the fold without hesitation.

"Well, Liam wasn't kidding." Jessie followed her niece the short distance between the foyer into the living room. "This looks more like a wedding shop than a living room."

Callie's round, pretty face was alight with excitement over her wedding. Her fiancé, Tony Jr., was a young man living with an intellectual disability who had fallen in love and proposed to Callie. At first, Kate and Tony Jr.'s parents were skeptical, certain that the relationship would fizzle. But it never had, and the duo were madly in love.

Kate gave Jessie a strong, quick hug. "That man is always exaggerating."

Kate was a natural beauty, with a lean, muscular build and brown hair with blond streaks from time out in the sun. Her skin was always tanned with sun freckles smattered across the bridge of her thin nose and across her cheeks.

With her hands on her hips, Jessie shook her head. "Not this time."

The modest living room was filled to the brim with dresses, presents, an ornate cake-topper, bridal magazines piled everywhere and accessories for the bridal party. Callie had always wanted to be a summer bride. While she had had to wait a few years for Tony's parents, Tottie and Tony Salviano Sr., to wrap up their lives in California and move to a small hobby ranch a stone's throw from the Triple K, her dream of being a summer bride was coming true.

Callie grabbed Jessie's hand and pulled her excitedly to the master bedroom she would be occupying with her soon-to-be husband. Kate followed along.

"Look!" Her niece unzipped a large black garment bag. "It's my d-dress!"

Inside the garment bag hung a snow-white ball gown with a tulle skirt, a satin bodice, satin-covered buttons down the back, a sweetheart neckline and cap sleeves. The tulle skirt had hand-sewn crystals, which would make Callie sparkle as she walked down the aisle.

"Oh, Callie." Jessie felt her eyes tear up with happiness for her niece. "It's more beautiful than I remember."

As Callie's maid of honor, Jessie had been there to help her niece pick out a dress.

"And here's the veil." Kate showed her the veil that was covered in the same crystals as the skirt of her ball gown.

"Wait!" Callie suddenly exclaimed. "I—I need to get my tiara!"

"Princess Calico," Kate said, and Jessie could see the emotion in her sister-in-law's eyes. There was a lot of happiness mixed with some sadness for the change that was coming.

"I knew she was going to go full-on princess." Jessie laughed. Even though Callie had been raised on a ranch and was a talented equestrian who had competed, and won, in the Special Olympics, she was also a total girlie girl.

Callie raced back into the bedroom, her cheeks flushed with excitement, but this time she had donned an ornate crown encrusted with crystals.

"See my t-tiara?"

Jessie smiled at her. "That's not a tiara."

"Yes, i-it i-is." Callie frowned at her.

"That's a crown fit for a queen, not a princess."

That made Callie giggle happily, duck her head and throw herself into Jessie's body for a long hug.

"I—I'm a queen." Callie spun around in a circle, her arms stretched out wide like she was about to take flight. "Queen Callie!"

"Lord have mercy." Kate put the veil back for safe keeping until the wedding date. "Let's go show Jessie her dress."

Callie squealed, clapped her hands together and raced back out of the bedroom.

"I hope my belly fits in my dress on Callie's big day." Jessie ran her hand over her growing baby bump.

"I am so sorry! I should have congratulated you right off the bat," Kate apologized, her expression embarrassed.

"No." Jessie shook her head. "You've got so much on your plate right now. I didn't expect you to remember."

"Well, thank you for understanding." Kate hugged her. "And congratulations."

"Thank you," Jessie said. "It was a bit of a shock, but we're really happy about it."

"This i-is your dress." Callie took a champagne colored dress off a nearby clothing rack. The dress had a tulle skirt, with a sweetheart neckline that mirrored Callie's dress. It had an empire waist, so no reason to worry about the fit down the road.

"It's beautiful. I love it," Jessie said, touching the skirt carefully.

Callie nodded her agreement. "Hawk can w-walk you down the aisle."

"You didn't have to do that, Callie!"

"I—I wanted to." Callie gave her a broad smile. "Dad says that you're going to have a b-baby."

"Yes, I am," Jessie said with a smile on her face.

Callie bent over so her face was level with Jessie's stomach. "Hi, b-baby."

When the younger bride-to-be was upright again, she said, "I—I'm having a b-baby with Tony."

Kate and Jessie exchanged a look. "We're still talking about that, Callie, remember?"

"I—I remember." Her niece nodded as she flung her long brown hair over her shoulder dramatically. "I—I can only have a b-baby after I—I'm married."

Kate made an obvious attempt to change the subject away from babies to safer topics when she asked, "Are you hungry? Callie just iced one of her famous chocolate cakes."

"Is that the sugary, buttery goodness I smelled when I walked in? My stomach started growling at me the minute I came through the front door," Jessie said. "We were on our way to lunch in town when my mom summoned me to the ranch for a talk."

"Fun," Kate said facetiously.

"So much fun." Jessie laughed. "But I think we actually made a little bit of progress with Dad."

"Well, that's good." Her sister-in-law nodded. "Jock can be stubborn, but he loves you."

"Sometimes too much I think." Jessie sat down at the small round dining table with Kate, while Callie, still wearing her crown, brought a plate with a large slice of her chocolate cake from the kitchen. Callie was an accomplished cook and had started an online business called Callie's Cookies & Cakes. It was a hit, and the business was doing well enough for her to support herself financially.

"Oh, my goodness." Jessie had taken a fork out of the Mason jar in the center of the table; Kate always stored her silverware that way. "This is amazing."

Callie brought coffee and flavored creamer to the table before she sat down with them. "Dark chocolate, gluten free. My b-bestseller."

"None for me." Jessie refused the coffee but took another big bite of the cake. "This is absolutely decadent."

"Thank you." Callie tilted her head to the side, grinning happily at the compliment as her rounded cheeks turned pink beneath her ivory skin.

Callie's phone rang. "It's Tony!"

Callie disappeared into the back of the house to her former bedroom. When she moved from the house on the hill into this 1970s ranch, she and Tony would occupy the master bedroom.

"Almost there." Jessie took another bite of the scrumptious, decadent cake Callie had made.

"Three years in the making," Kate said, the area around her eyes and mouth showing fatigue. "I'm going to be relieved to get us through the wedding, finally, but the truth is, that's when the real work will begin. Especially when Callie keeps on pushing to have a baby." Kate paused for a second. "At least Tony Jr. is being reasonable about this. He tells her all the time that he isn't ready to be a father. I hope he tells her that for the next thirty or forty years."

Jessie nodded, wanting to be a sounding board for Kate; her sister-in-law appeared to need it.

"Six people in a marriage will be tough," Kate said, referring to the fact that both sets of parents also had to be closely involved in the marriage. Despite their accomplishments, neither Tony nor Callie could live on their own without support from family, friends and adults in the community trained to work with individuals with disabilities.

"I'm sure it will be, but you'll figure it out." Jessie struck an encouraging tone. "At least her business is booming."

"She's so creative and ambitious," her sister-in-law said. "She still can't do basic math problems, which makes money management a full-time job for me, but I couldn't be more proud of her."

The two of them chatted for a while longer before Jessie brought up the original reason for her visit. By then, Callie was off the phone with her fiancé and had returned to the table still wearing her sparkling crown.

"So, I do have something that I need to ask you both," Jessie said. "How would you feel about Hawk and me getting married sometime during the rehearsal dinner night at the Sugar Creek main house? Mama suggested it, and it seemed like a decent idea at the time. What do you think?"

Kate shrugged a shoulder. "I don't mind at all. Callie?"

A broad smile came across Callie's face, and her blue eyes lit up with happiness. "I—I think i-it's a great idea. Can I—I be your maid of honor?"

"Of course you can." Jessie held out her arms to Callie. "How did you get to be such a sweet, sweet girl, Callie?"

Callie giggled behind her hand before she said, "I—I was b-born this way."

At the end of their visit, Kate walked her to the door.

Jessie hugged her tightly. "Thank you again for letting us crash the rehearsal dinner. I owe you one. A big one."

Kate leaned against the doorjamb, her hands tucked into front pockets of her faded figure-hugging jeans. "You know, there is something you could do for me…"

"Name it."

"Would you *please* ask Hawk to stop encouraging Liam to use the word *crikey*?"

Jessie parked her Jeep in front of Bruce and Savannah's whitewashed farmhouse after her visit with Kate and Callie.

"Guess what?" Jessie asked her fiancé.

Hawk was sitting in a wooden rocking chair on Bruce and Savannah's covered porch with several of the dogs from the larger pack keeping him company.

Jessie plucked his phone out of his hand playfully and then sat down on his lap and curled her body into his. He immediately wrapped his arms around her body, kissed her deeply on the lips and then asked, "What?"

"We—" she kissed him lightly on the lips again "—have a wedding date."

"Kate and Callie said yes?"

"Kate and Callie said yes."

"That's good news, then." Hawk held on to her legs to keep her on his lap as he gently rocked them back and forth.

"I'll be a June bride." She laid her head on his shoulder, breathing in the familiar scent of his skin.

"I like the sound of that, Mrs. Bowhill."

"Brand-Bowhill," she corrected.

"As you wish."

Jessie lifted her head so she could look at his handsome face. "Did you have a good time with Bruce?"

"It was brilliant, yeah. It was great to get back in the saddle. It took some getting used to, I'll admit. Wish I had thought to bring my own saddle along. But being out there mustering cows with a good mate was exactly what the doctor ordered for me."

"I'm glad."

Hawk nodded, and she could tell that he had something else he wanted to say but was hesitating to say it.

"What?" she asked.

"Getting back to work got me thinking…" He stopped rocking the chair. "I think I'd like to stay around here."

Jessie leaned back a bit. "You mean not go on our trip?"

"If Sugar Creek is going to be my new home, I want to get to know her better. We could take some horses and camp out by that stream of yours and make some plans for the future."

"So, let me get this straight." Jessie cocked her head to the side. "You want me to trade my luxury accommodations—comfy beds, room service, spas, hot tubs—that I booked for us and sleep on the ground in a tent?"

"I'll be in that swag with you, which sweetens the deal, I should think."

"I must really love you," she teased. "I'll cancel our reservations right after dinner."

Hawk gave her a long kiss as a thank-you. They were still locked in a romantic embrace when Savannah opened the screen door, wiping her hands on a dish towel. "Time to come up for air, you two. Dinner is served."

Chapter Seven

When Hunter, one of her seven older brothers, drove into the clearing at Liam's cabin, Jessie ran down the steps to greet him. Hawk, who needed to keep himself busy almost every waking hour of the day, was in the barn fixing anything broken with materials he found on the property.

"Thank you so much for letting us borrow your rig!" Jessie gave Hunter a hug when he got out of the truck.

Hunter—with his tall, dark hair, deeply tanned skin, hawkish nose and deep-set blue eyes—could have been her twin. He was *her* in a male body.

Her brother handed her the keys to his super-duty truck and his horse trailer. "Not a problem, sis."

"Hi, Dream," Jessie greeted one of the horses in the trailer. "I've missed you."

Dream Chaser had been her barrel racing horse for years—they had traveled many miles together—but lately she had been a trail riding horse for Hunter's big city wife, Skyler. Dream had been living on a nearby farm that Hunter had purchased from his childhood friend.

"You're sure Skyler doesn't mind me having Dream for a while?"

"She's fine with it. She'll miss her, but she knows how much she means to you," Hunter said. "It's actually pretty good timing, because Skyler's taking classes this summer and doesn't have as much time to spend with Dream as she'd like."

"Okay. That makes me feel better, at least."

"And Zodiac will be a good trail horse for Hawk," her brother said of the second horse in the trailer. "He's sure-footed and knows the terrain."

They walked around to the other side of the trailer, where Hunter opened a door that led to the efficiency apartment built in front.

"Everything in here is good to go. You have plenty of propane, the battery is fully charged from the solar panels on the top of this rig." Her brother stepped up into the apartment. "You have everything you guys will need—bathroom, kitchen, king-size bed in the bulkhead. You'll have to stock up the kitchen, but other than that, you're set for a while."

"It's perfect," she said, looking around. "This is a good compromise. I like a bed and Hawk prefers to sleep outside on the hard ground."

Hunter smiled at that. "Can't say that I blame him."

"Of course you can't," she said. Hunter was as much of a dyed-in-the-wool cowboy as Hawk; and it was that commonality that made Jessie believe that Hawk would be able to relate to Hunter in the same way he did Bruce.

Jessie walked with her brother over to the barn, where Hawk was breaking a sweat fixing one of the stall gates that had rusted off its hinges. And as she suspected, Hunter and Hawk hit it off like gangbusters, talking about cattle and horses and dirt bikes.

"I heard you helped Bruce move some cows yesterday," Hunter said.

"It was a bloody good time, I'll say that. The saddle's gonna take getting used to, but it reminded me of being back home, for sure." Hawk wiped the sweat off his brow with the sleeve of his button-down cotton shirt before he readjusted his hat.

There was something about the fact that he was choosing to wear his Australian hat instead of the Stetson she had purchased for him that struck her as an outward sign of a bigger issue inside her husband-to-be's heart. Yes, he seemed to be eager to throw himself into life at Sugar Creek, but her analytical side believed that just maybe he was trying to distract himself from missing home.

"We could always use a set of hands around here," Hunter said. "And you don't have to be trained."

Hawk smiled at that. "I could probably learn a few new tricks. There's always more than one way of doing something, I suppose."

"That's a two-way street," Hunter said.

"I reckon that's right."

Her brother and her fiancé talked for a while longer before they parted ways with a promise to touch base after they returned from their staycation on the ranch.

"Do you want to help me load some things into the trailer?" she asked.

"Absolutely." Hawk leaned over and gave her a kiss. "Let me just finish this up, and I'll be there straight-away."

Jessie headed down the wide dirt aisle of the barn; at the entrance, she turned around and looked at Hawk, her hand naturally going to her baby bump. Every day, she felt closer to the child growing inside her; every day she fell just a little bit more in love with her Australian cowboy. She only hoped that life with her and their child would be enough to overcome any feelings of regret that Hawk may have about leaving behind his life in the Australian outback.

"Are you okay?" Hawk had noticed that she was watching him.

"Just admiring you," she said. "Can't I admire you?"

Hawk flashed that smile of his and flexed one of

his arms. "Of course you can. Let me give you a bit of a show."

"I love you." She laughed.

"I love you," he said with a wink. "Now, if you've had enough of a cheeky look, I need to finish my work."

On her way back to the cabin, Jessie couldn't shake the doubt she had rattling around in her head that there was something off with her fiancé. But while part of her wanted to know what he was keeping from her, there was an even larger part that wanted to be kept completely in the dark. What was going on in Hawk's head would affect them both—and their baby too.

Jessie jogged up the porch steps and headed straight to the kitchen to pack up the groceries they had purchased earlier that morning. She was loaded down with two heavy bags on each arm when Hawk met her at the bottom of the stairs.

"Where are we going to store all of this food?" he asked.

"You'll see."

Hawk took the bags from her and followed her around to the other side of the trailer. She opened the door to the small apartment built into the front half, took the two small steps up into the space and turned around in time to see the pure look of shock on Hawk's face.

"What have you got here?" he asked her, his eyes taking in the space.

"A few creature comforts."

"A few?" He set the bags down on the bench seat.

"I think this is a good compromise." She wrapped her arms around him and tilted her head back for a kiss. "You get to explore Sugar Creek, and I get to take a hot shower. Win, win."

Hawk never missed an opportunity to kiss her. After a flirty kiss, he asked, "I suppose you want me to sleep in that bed, do you?"

"Well—" she slipped her hands downward to his rear end and squeezed "—I hope we won't just be sleeping on this trip."

"I need to get my beauty sleep if I'm going to keep up with you."

"Hawk Bowhill, you are pretty enough."

After stealing a couple more kisses, Hawk said, "How about this for a deal? I'll sleep with you in that bed if one or two times you slip into my swag with me."

Jessie had been introduced to Hawk's uniquely Australian tent that looked like a cross between a tent and a sleeping bag. She couldn't be completely sure, but that cozy swag of his may have just been the place where their baby was conceived.

She kissed him on the cheek. "Deal."

There was a door right past the bathroom that led directly to the horses. While Hawk grabbed a few of his things, including his canvas swag, Jessie checked on Dream and Zodiac.

"How are they going?" Hawk asked her as he threw his swag into the back of Hunter's truck.

"I think they're getting restless." Jessie shut the door to the sleeping quarters tightly. "Are we ready?"

"I think so."

They both climbed into the truck, and Jessie cranked the engine.

"Are you excited?" she asked him.

"Yeah, I think I am."

"So am I." Jessie slipped on a pair of sunglasses, shifted into gear, and headed toward one of the more traveled back roads on the property. "I think I'm going to really enjoy showing you the ranch and see it anew through your eyes."

"Better than a fancy hotel, do you reckon?"

Jessie smiled at him. "I *was* really looking forward to a couple's massage and room service."

"I don't mind giving your shoulders a rub." Hawk hung his arm out of the open window.

"Wow." Jessie laughed. "How can I refuse that kind of offer?"

Hawk was doing his best to keep his mind in Montana. But it was difficult. His grandfather was still healthy and vibrant at the age of eighty-one and still kept a tight grip on Daintree Downs, so Hawk knew, in his heart if not his mind, that the station was in good hands. But he missed it. He missed the landscape, his horses, his small crew of musterers and his way of life. He had spent more time sleeping outdoors in his life than indoors. A bed, no matter how hard the mattress, felt too soft.

"Let's take the horses up to that lookout point," Jessie said, her silky brown-black hair plaited into a long single braid.

Day by day, Hawk fell more in love with Jessie. He loved her laugh, her smile and her beautiful spirit. Of course, she was beautiful on the outside too, with her willowy body that was subtle in its shapeliness. Her breasts were on the small side, but they fit her athletic frame perfectly. But he'd always cared less about the outward appearance—not that he didn't like a good-looking *sheila* the same as the next bloke, but any woman who wore makeup every day or went for weekly spa treatments would not make it in the outback. Jessie was gorgeous, but she was also an authentic American cowgirl. She didn't shy away from getting her hands dirty or jumping in to help with a cow giving birth. For Hawk, she was the perfect woman. In his mind, Jessie was made just for him. And in turn, he was made just for her.

"Hawk?" Jessie asked when she walked over to where he was standing. "Did you hear me?"

Hawk hooked his arm around her shoulders and pulled her toward him. "I heard you."

He looked down into his fiancée's pretty upturned face, and he was immediately drawn into her sky blue eyes. Just one look into those eyes, and he was put under Jessie's spell. It had been that way from the first meeting; he reckoned it would always be that way.

"Where did you go?" she asked him, her hand resting on his chest directly over his heart. "You looked like you were a million miles away."

"I was just taking in the beauty of this place," he said. And even if he had been miles away at Daintree Downs, that was true. There were many places in Australia that resembled Montana, but Queensland—called the Sunshine State for its tropical climate—wasn't one of them. Much like Florida in the States, Queensland grew palm trees. But with a decade of drought, the landscape at Daintree looked burnt. Everything looked thirsty.

"I'm glad you think so." She smiled up at him, and he felt his mood lighten when he saw those two pretty little dimples in her cheeks.

"I'd like you to show me some building sites." Hawk gave her a kiss before he let her go.

"We have so many choices," Jessie said enthusiastically. "You will be the one to select where we will build our house."

"We should make that decision together."

"You'll pick," she said over her shoulder as she disappeared into the living quarters in the trailer.

Hawk laughed, knowing that there was no sense in arguing with her. She could be just as stubborn as Jock—a family trait he realized. He would pick the building site if she wanted, but he would pay close attention to her favorite spot, and even if that wasn't his favorite, that would be the spot that he chose.

Hawk unlatched the trailer doors and lowered the ramp for the horses to back out.

"Here comes Dream," Jessie said from inside the trailer.

"There's a good girl," Hawk said as the horse felt behind its body cautiously to find footing. Dream slowly backed out of the trailer; Hawk caught the lead rope Jessie had clipped to the horse's halter, led her to a small ring on the side of the trailer and looped the lead rope though the ring in order to keep Dream from wandering off to forage the abundant foliage nearby.

"Ready for Zodiac?" Jessie called out.

"Ready."

Hawk gave the gelding a pat on the back as it carefully backed down the ramp of the trailer.

"He's a real looker, isn't he?" Zodiac was a flashy black-and-white paint horse with bright blue eyes and a black-and-white mane and tail.

"Yes, he is." Jessie opened the tack room door located near the entrance to the living quarters. "And he knows it too. But he's more than just a pretty face. He's a great little trail pony. Sure-footed and fit."

"Can't ask for more than that." Hawk ran his hand over the horse's muscular neck, back and rounded hindquarters. Zodiac was a well-bred quarter horse, so he had thickly muscled, powerful hindquarters, perfect for cutting cattle from a larger herd.

"Okay," Jessie said with a secretive smile on her face, "close your eyes."

"Close my eyes?" he repeated, caught off guard by the request.

"Yes." She continued to smile at him. "Close your eyes."

Hawk did as he was told until he heard her say, "Now open them."

Hawk opened his eyes, and it took him a second to realize that Jessie had an Australian saddle in her arms.

"Where'd you get that?"

"My brother Noah used to collect saddles when he was younger. He let me borrow it."

"That's a bloody nice saddle." Hawk stepped closer to look over the finely crafted Aussie saddle.

"It's yours until we can get you one of your own."

"Thank you." Hawk kissed her again. Jessie really cared about his happiness. Yes, they had debated for months about which country to live in to start their married lives. But if she really knew that he was walking away from his inheritance to be with her in Montana, she would insist that they go back to Australia. And then she would be a new mother, raising a newborn away from her mother and extended family; she would feel isolated and, he worried, lonely and depressed.

"I surprised you," she said happily, handing him a saddle pad from the tack room.

"You've always surprised me." Hawk threw the

saddle pad onto Zodiac's back and then put the Aussie saddle on top of it.

They finished tacking up the horses and headed across the ripe pastureland toward the raw woodland. They traveled slowly through the woods, letting the horses find their footing across layers of fallen leaves, downed branches and hidden rocks. They ducked beneath low-hanging branches, winding their way toward the stream, where the horses had a chance to drink from the cool, babbling water before they traversed across the stream to the other side.

"I want to take you to an outlook before I go to the first building site," Jessie called back to him.

"Sounds good."

Being in an Aussie saddle made him feel more at ease and more at home. For him, the horn on a Western saddle just got in his way. And he had cracked his family jewels on them several times when he was riding with Bruce.

At first, the hill was gradual, but halfway up to the peak, the grade became steeper. Hawk leaned forward slightly to help Zodiac keep his balance and gave the horse his head by loosening the reins. Ahead, Dream stumbled several times on jagged rocks.

"How are you going?" Hawk called up to Jessie.

"We're okay," Jessie said. "Dream has shallow hooves, so those rocks really give her a hard time. But she always gets me there safe and sound."

They reached the peak of the small mountain, and the sun, which was filtered through the leaves and branches of the thick forest trees, shone down on his face. He adjusted the brim of his old hat, faithful through many years of work, and followed Jessie to a good spot to dismount.

"Will you look at that view?" Hawk exclaimed sincerely. From his limited experience with Montana, he'd always been looking from lower ground to the peaks of faraway mountains. For the first time, he was getting a look at the land from the vantage of a mountaintop.

Jessie smiled at him, her pretty face beaming from the ride and his unvarnished appreciation of the view. They tied the horses to a nearby tree, and the two trail ponies immediately began to nibble on the tree leaves. Holding hands, Jessie and Hawk climbed the short distance to the rocky face of the mountain, where there were only a few trees that had managed to grow within the rocky crevices.

At the peak, they stood together in silence; he loved the feel of the cool breeze on his warmed face. There was a sweet scent of pine in the air, and the only sound he heard came from the birds flying nearby.

"Wow," Hawk said, truly awed by the land that Jessie loved so dearly.

"Everything the eye can see is Sugar Creek land." She pointed ahead of them. "You can see the main house in the distance."

In comparison, the best way to see Daintree's land holdings was to view it from a helicopter, but, more so than any other time, Hawk understood the magnitude of his love's connection to this land.

Together, they sat on the rock face and shared a bottle of water.

"Do you love it?" Jessie asked after a long stretch of silence.

Hawk was happy that he could give her the truthful response that she wanted. "Yes, I do."

"I knew you would!" She threw her arms around him happily. "I knew that once you got here, you would fall in love with it!"

"I love it, and I love you."

"I love you more," Jessie said, her face beaming with happiness.

"Not possible." He kissed her again, loving the feel of her soft lips against his.

Jessie hugged him tightly and rested her head against his chest. They stood there together enjoying the intermittent gusts of wind rustled through the leaves on the trees below them.

"Are you ready to go?" Jessie asked.

"I reckon so."

"Good!" Jessie grabbed his hand, and they headed back to the horses. "Next stop, the first building site."

"Lead the way."

"Here are the vegetables." Jessie carried a bowl of prepped vegetables out to Hawk.

"Brilliant." Hawk looked up. "Just dump them right into the pot."

Hawk had set up a cast-iron pot over the open flame of the fire. *Roughing it*—sleeping on the ground, cooking over a fire, far away from civilization, no running water, no electronics—for her man. In fact, during his short time in Montana, this was the first moment that she saw her Australian outback cowboy looking completely at home and happy. Now she was glad that he'd suggested exploring their future homestead at Sugar Creek—Hawk wouldn't have enjoyed any sightseeing more than camping out.

Jessie leaned back against a log Hawk had dragged over to where he had created a firepit, her legs stretched out, ankles crossed, and her hands resting on her baby bump.

"I'm looking forward to feeling the baby. I heard it feels like butterflies."

Hawk finished stirring the beef stew cooking over the flame before he joined her. He sat down beside her and put his arms around her shoulders.

"I thought I was the one who gave you butterflies in your stomach."

She cuddled up next to him. "You *always* give me butterflies, handsome. This is your doing."

The fire crackled and popped as the sun set; the early evening sky was painted with strokes of deep purple, burnt orange and light shades of pink.

"Did you have a good day?" she asked, wishing she didn't feel so insecure about Hawk's happiness.

Hawk kissed the top of her head. "Every day with you is a good day for me."

"Even when we disagree?"

"Even when we disagree."

Content in his arms, Jessie breathed in and let the breath out on a long, happy sigh.

"We may be able to find out the gender during our next appointment," she told him. "Do you want to know?"

"That's your call, I should think."

"Well, it's really *our* decision," she said. "Savannah asked me if I wanted to have a joint gender-reveal party."

"We don't have many of those out in the bush."

She laughed. "No. Probably not. Would you be open to it?"

"Sure, I am," Hawk said, getting up to check on the stew. "Sounds like a good bit of fun."

Jessie sat upright, curled her knees upward and clasped her hands together on her shins. "Do you want a boy or a girl? And don't say *healthy*, because that's a given. Boy or girl? Go!"

"Girl," he said, joining her again, "for a start. And then a boy."

"I like the sound of that." Jessie looked into his eyes. "One of each."

Hawk took off his hat so he could kiss her more easily. "Have I told you lately that I love you?"

"Yes," she said, keeping her lips close to his for more of his sweet kisses. "But tell me again."

Chapter Eight

The week they spent exploring their one hundred-acre homestead was magical. Insulated from the world, Jessie felt as if they were able to reconnect and find their way back to the couple they had been in Australia.

"It's our last night," Jessie said, soaking up the warmth of the fire Hawk had just built for them.

"It's flown by for me."

"Me too."

Instead of sitting down beside her, Hawk held out his hand for her. "How's about a dance, gorgeous?"

Even though Hawk was a rugged, masculine man, something she truly loved about him, he had a wonderful soft romantic side that never ceased to surprise her.

She slipped her hand into his, and he helped her to a stand. Hawk put one hand on her waist and extended the other.

"Don't we need music?" she asked with a laugh.

"No," he said, twirling her around. "We make our own music."

They danced beneath a three-quarter moon until they were out of breath from laughing. Hawk dipped her one last time, brought her upright and then kissed her in a way that let her know that dinner would be delayed. They had slept most nights in the trailer living quarters, but tonight, she would join him, as promised, in his swag.

Silently, Hawk stripped her T-shirt off her body and made short work of her bra. Her breasts had begun to get tender during her pregnancy, and Hawk's hand massaging her naked breast felt so good that she closed her eyes and moaned with pleasure. When his lips captured her nipple and suckled, she felt her knees go weak. She held on to his shoulders, closed her eyes and let desire wash over her entire body.

Hawk knelt down before her and kissed her baby bump before pulling off one of her boots after another. Then Hawk did a quick job of unbuttoning and unzipping her jeans and pushing them and her simple cotton underpants down to her ankles. She stepped out of her clothes and stood naked by the fire. Hawk's eyes swept possessively over her body, and Jessie loved the way he admired her. She felt like the only woman in the world when Hawk looked at her the way her was looking at her now.

"My turn," Jessie said playfully, quickly unbuttoning his standard cotton plaid button-down shirt. She pushed it off his shoulders so she could run her hands over his sculpted chest and abs. She dropped flirty kissed on his neck and chest while her hands opened the zipper of his faded jeans.

"Too bloody slow." Hawk stepped backward, yanked off his boots, stripped out of his jeans and underwear.

Her eyes naturally traveled the length of his body, which was lean and fit from years of hard work on the farm. His shoulders were broad with thick muscle. Her gaze stopped and lingered on his erection. When her eyes traveled back up to his, he was looking at her like a predator studies its prey.

Hawk scooped her up into his arms and carried her to his swag. The moment he laid her down on her back and without foreplay, Hawk was inside her, buried deep. He held her hands above her head, entwined with his as he took her on a wonderful ride. He knew her body like a concert pianist knew a piano. Every thrust, every kiss, was designed to bring her more pleasure than she thought possible.

"I love you, Jess." Hawk's breath on her ear made her squirm with excitement.

"I love you!" These words came out breathy and quick, right before she cried out his name.

In the aftermath of their lovemaking, Hawk covered them with a sheet and pulled her back into his body, his arms around her waist, his hand on her small baby bump.

"I wish it could always be like this," Jessie murmured, her eyes closed. "Right now, we are the only two people in the world."

Hawk kissed her bare shoulder. "Remembering times like these will help us get through the rough patches."

"I hope so." Jessie snuggled closer to him.

"Don't hope," her fiancé murmured sleepily. "Know."

During the weeks that followed their camping trip, Jessie felt like a hamster running on a wheel. While Hawk kept busy with ranch work, she was making arrangements for their pop-up wedding ceremony the day of Callie's rehearsal dinner. Callie's soon-to-be in-laws were Catholic and wanted a church ceremony; Kate had raised Callie to believe in God but did not subscribe to any organized religion. The families had agreed to compromise on a ceremony in a local Unitarian nondenominational church. The priest of the church agreed to marry Hawk and her in a no-frills quick nuptial prior to the rehearsal of Callie's ceremony.

"Bruce is taking Hawk to get a suit tomorrow, so he'll be set." Jessie pushed a shopping cart down the aisle at the local grocery store. "Now I just need to figure out what I'm going to wear."

Savannah was walking beside her, selecting things from the shelves and putting them in the basket. Both of them had recent ultrasounds that had confirmed the gender of their babies, and now they were preparing for their joint gender-reveal party, which would be held at Savannah and Bruce's farmhouse. Each of them had ordered a cake, had given the cake shop the envelope with the genders, and when they cut the cakes, it would either be pink or blue on the inside.

"Why don't you borrow my dress?"

"Seriously?" Jessie asked. Lilly had handcrafted an incredible wedding dress in the tradition of the Chippewa Cree for Savannah. The dress was covered in small silver bells that had tinkled with joy as Savannah had walked down the aisle at her vow renewal ceremony at the Story Mansion in downtown Bozeman.

"Of course," Savannah said. "Something old, something new, something borrowed, something blue…"

Jessie looked down at her own body. "I'm not sure the dress would hit me right. I'm a lot taller than you."

"I think it'll work." Her sister-in-law put some hamburger buns in the cart. "When we get back to the ranch, you can try it on."

Jessie helped Savannah put away the groceries for their joint gender-reveal party with a promise to help get the house ready the day of the party. Still foremost on her mind was the fact that her father was staunchly opposed to her marriage, and he had barely spoken two words to her since their last meeting. In truth, she was concerned that Jock would refuse to attend the gender-reveal party; Jessie hated the idea that her issues with her father could negatively impact Savannah's day as well.

"I honestly don't know if he'll even attend." Jessie shared her worries with her sister-in-law. "Mom only has so much influence."

"Just go talk with him. Be the first to break the ice." Savannah pulled a garment bag out of her walk-in closet and laid the bag across the king-size bed. "Take the ultrasound pictures with you. You know how much Jock loves his grandchildren. He's always wanted the main house to be bursting at the seams with Brands."

Savannah carefully unzipped the garment bag to reveal the handmade wedding dress housed within.

As she pushed the bag aside to expose more of the dress, her sister-in-law continued, "Most men hate to admit that they are wrong—the Brand men in particular are *horrible* about it. Give Dad a way to change his mind without admitting he might have overreacted."

"It's worth a try I suppose," she said, her tone less than confident.

"Of course it is," Savannah answered. "You are Jock's pride and joy. Help him find a path back to you that doesn't bruise his ego."

"Now—" Savannah held the dress up in front of Jessie's body "—I think this will look incredible on you."

Jessie felt afraid to even touch the precious dress. "Oh, Savannah. It's the most beautiful dress I've ever seen in my life. If I hadn't sprung all of this on Mom, I know she would have made one for me."

"It would be meaningful for me to have you wear mine." Savannah led her over to a full-length mirror.

Jessie stared at her reflection. "If I wear this, there would be enough room for my baby belly."

Savannah smiled at her. "You don't even look pregnant."

"I know," she agreed. "I look like I had a few large meals. But he or she is in there."

Both of them turned their attention back to the mirror. Jessie asked, "Are you sure, Savannah?"

"One hundred percent." Savannah's green eyes were shining with anticipation. "I *can't wait* to see it on you. Let's try it on!"

Jessie gave Savannah a bear hug. "You're the best sister-in-law ever!"

A pleased smile brightened Savannah's pretty face. "Don't say that too loudly! Lord help you, you have seven sisters-in-laws."

With Savannah's help, Jessie carefully stepped into the custom dress.

"Will it zip?" she asked expectantly.

"Of course it will zip," Savannah said and Jessie was happy to hear that satisfying sound of a zipper being easily zipped closed.

"Well?" her sister-in-law asked when Jessie looked at her reflection in the mirror. "What do you think?"

The dress hit her well above her knee and it didn't work with her baby bump. Disappointed, Jessie frowned at her reflection.

"No go." Jessie shrugged her shoulders. "Legs are too long, belly is too big."

"Well, first," her sister-in-law said, her arm supportively around her shoulders, "legs are never too long! And, second, we will find the very best dress to showcase your beautiful belly."

Feeling better, Jessie hugged her sister-in-law tightly. "What did I say? My absolute favorite!"

"Thank you, Savannah. For everything," Jessie said as they walked out onto the porch.

"That's what family's for."

They walked down the steps together and headed toward Savannah's mint green Ford Bronco parked a few feet away. The Bronco had been an anniversary gift from Bruce, and it fit Savannah's personality perfectly: both feminine and strong.

Savannah's daughter had been visiting with Lilly while they went shopping, and Savannah was going to drop Jessie off at Liam's cabin on her way to pick her up. Jessie was about to get into the passenger side when a large industrial-sized tractor, one of many at Sugar Creek, rounded a curve and headed toward them.

"Hey! That's Hawk!"

Savannah stepped back out of the Bronco and put

her hand above her eyes to stop the glare of the sun from blurring her vision.

With a laugh, Savannah said, "Making himself right at home. That's great news."

Jessie ran around the back of the Bronco to hug Savannah. "I'm going to hitch a ride with my cowboy."

Jessie bolted to the road and held out her thumb as if she were hitchhiking. Hawk, who knew his way around industrial tractors, looked happy and at ease behind the wheel. He was driving one of the newer models in Sugar Creek's vast equipment holdings; on the front of the tractor, large arms were holding an enormous round hay bale to put in one of the pastures.

Hawk braked and opened the door of the enclosed climate-controlled cab. "Heading my way, gorgeous?"

"You bet I am!"

Hawk waved at his soon-to-be sister-in-law. "G'day, Savannah!"

"G'day, Hawk!" Savannah called out with a wave of her own.

Jessie easily navigated the step up to the tractor compartment. She took Hawk's outstretched hand. Hawk kissed her the moment she was close enough.

"I'm happy to see you!" she said to Hawk as she sat down on a small jump seat next to the driver in the cab and closed the door.

"I was hoping I'd find you here," Hawk said, cranking the engine. "I've got all the luck."

They both waved at Savannah as they headed farther down the road.

"Kate can't get Liam to stop saying *crikey*, and now Savannah is saying *g'day*. You're *Aussifying* my family."

"It's all just a bit of fun," Hawk said with a smile.

"I actually *secretly* love it." She leaned her body toward his, bumping his shoulder with hers affectionately. "But, Kate? She's on the other side of that argument."

"How have you been going today?" Hawk asked, steering with one hand and holding her hand with the other.

"Good, really. We got everything we need for the party this weekend. And the bakery agreed to put a rush on our cakes because we've been using them for years. Plus, we ordered two cakes instead of one."

"Have you changed your prediction?" Hawk glanced over at her, his eyes full of love.

"Nope. I think it's a boy." She shook her head. "I know you think it's a girl."

"I'm keen to find out either way."

"Me too! I had no idea how difficult it was going to be waiting even a week. I keep having to stop myself from calling the doctor's office."

As they always did, they chatted all the way to the pasture and kept right on talking on their way back to the barn, where the tractor would be dropped off and refueled if necessary. Hawk, to Jessie's relief, seemed in much better spirits after a day spent working on the ranch. He was a man used to hard work; that ethic was ingrained in him since he was a young boy. Even though Sugar Creek wasn't Daintree Downs, there was always plenty that needed to be done. One thing Hawk wouldn't do without in Montana was ample farm work—similar to what could be found on his own cattle station. She hoped it would make his transition easier.

After dropping off the tractor, Hawk got behind the wheel of her car.

"I've been thinking about names while I was working today," he said to her as he cranked the engine and shifted into Drive.

"Oh, yeah?" she asked with a playful combativeness in her tone. "Bring it, Bowhill."

They disagreed on their predictions for the gender of the baby *and* names for either a girl or a boy.

"Greyson Pengana Bowhill for a boy or a girl."

"Have you been breathing too many diesel fumes?" she asked, her brows lifted in surprise.

"Don't strike it down before you've given it a chance to sink in."

"Oh, don't worry, it's sunk in," Jessie said. "And it made me feel a bit queasy."

"Are you sure that's not from the morning sickness?"

"Yes, I'm sure," she bantered. "I don't know what

was wrong with my idea to call our daughter Luna and our boy Leo. These are perfect names."

"Is it possible for *me* to have morning sickness? Now I feel a bit queasy."

Jessie punched him in the arm playfully. "One of us has to eventually win, you know. Baby can't come without a name."

"By the time *Grey* arrives, you'll have come to your senses." Hawk parked the Jeep.

"Is that so?" she asked.

"That's so."

With a smile, Jessie tilted up the brim of his hat, leaned over, and he met her halfway to exchange a kiss.

"Do you know what I think?" she asked while her hand ran suggestively up his thigh.

"What?" he asked, the look in eyes shifting quickly from teasing to sensual.

"The first one to the bedroom gets to pick the name."

Laughing, Jessie quickly jumped out of the Jeep and raced for the steps. Hot on her heels, Hawk caught up with her in the living room, swept her up in his arms, and took them straight to the bedroom.

Desire had turned his striking eyes a dark shade of forest green; Hawk quickly shrugged out of his shirt and began to make short work of his boots and jeans. "Call it a tie?"

"Okay, fine." Jessie yanked her T-shirt off. "But I'll get you next time."

Naked and aroused, Hawk helped strip her out of the rest of her clothes. "No need to wait, gorgeous. You can get all of me right now."

Laughing, they both fell back onto the bed.

"Hmm." Jessie nuzzled his neck. "You smell all sweaty and manly."

"You fancy that, do you?" Hawk asked, holding her close.

"It's a total turn-on."

"That's my cheeky girl." Her fiancé covered her body with his. "Now give me a kiss and tell me that you love me."

"I love you!" Jessie laughed, wrapping her limbs around Hawk's body, anticipating the joyful ride he was about to give her.

Hawk kissed her deep and long before he said with a rough, emotional resonance in his voice, "And that makes me the luckiest bloke in the world, I should think."

Later that day, Jessie found her mother in her greenhouse lovingly caring for her wide variety of flowers and plants. "Where's Dad?"

Lilly greeted her with a warm smile and a hug. "I believe he's at the main barn working with Isabella's new horse."

Jessie sat down at a small wrought iron café table Lilly had put in the greenhouse so she could sit among her greenery.

"I saw him. He's a good-looking horse."

"He is that." Her mother joined her at the table. "It's hard to believe that I was sitting at this very table with Noah when he told me about Isabella."

Noah had found out last year that he had fathered a daughter, Isabella, with his then-fiancé, Annika. It had been a shock, yes, but a happy one for the entire family. Now, he was happily married to his best-friend, Dr. Shayna Wade, who was now pregnant with their first child together.

"Now," Lilly continued, "I can hardly remember a time when she wasn't a part of the flock."

Jessie nodded her agreement.

"And what of your little one?" Her mother reached across the table to squeeze her hand.

Whenever Jessie thought about her baby, she could feel her face light up and her eyes shine with sheer happiness. In her mind, she did have that baby glow.

"All is well." Jessie pulled a wallet out of her back pocket, opened it and slid out a sonogram picture of the baby.

Lilly accepted the photo and studied it. Wordlessly, her mother stood up, tears in her eyes, and hugged her tightly.

"My baby is having a baby," she said.

When Lilly returned to her chair, Jessie had tears in her eyes as well. "I never thought that I would be a mother so young—or even at all, really. But, Mom, it feels so right with Hawk. I love him more than I could ever say in words."

"Soulmates."

"Yes," she said, "I never really believed in that, for me at least, but yes. He is my soulmate. And for both of us, love at first sight. One day I was heartbroken over Hudson, and then the next day, I met Hawk, and for the first time, I understood *why* Hudson broke up with me. We never had this," Jessie said, opening up to her mother in a way that felt natural and good. "I never felt a fraction for Hudson what I do for Pengana. I had no idea that I was on autopilot in that relationship. But I was. I was sleepwalking through my life, and then one look from Hawk and I woke up."

Lilly held on to her hand. "I'm so happy to hear that, Jessie. You deserve to be loved and cherished every second of every day."

"I have that with Hawk, Mama. I promise you I do."

Jessie reached forward to brush the teardrops from her mother's soft cheeks. "Why are you still crying?"

"You've grown up," her mother said simply. "I wasn't ready, I suppose."

They both stood up and embraced. And when they both felt sufficiently comforted, and their emotions had run their course, Jessie asked, "So, what else is new, Mama?"

Lilly beamed at her when she asked, "Did I tell you? Beauty is about to give birth."

Beauty was Lilly's prized Belted heifer, a giant cream-colored cow that her mother had competed and won with in competitions across Montana.

"I didn't realize that she was that close?"

"She is, and I'm so nervous, I can hardly sleep. I know we have hundreds of babies born on this ranch, but this is my first."

"It's special," Jessie said.

"Yes, it really is." Lilly hooked Jessie's arm with hers and walked her out. "Now, be gentle with your dear old dad, Jess. He's having a hard time with all of this, and emotions have never been easy for Jock."

"I will, Mama. I promise that I will."

Jessie found her father in the main barn, which was dedicated to many of the horses that had been bred and trained on Sugar Creek. In her childhood, working in this barn, she had dreamed of a husband she would have one day. In those dreams, her husband was always with her in this barn, breeding, raising and training the finest quarter horses in the Western United States.

"Hi, Daddy," Jessie greeted her father.

Jock was brushing the little buckskin gelding in the crosstie area. He looked up at her, squinted his eyes and pressed his lips together as if he were trying to stop himself from saying a word to her.

"He's real nice." She let the horse smell her hand before she patted him on the neck.

When he still didn't respond, Jessie took the sonogram picture out of her wallet and placed it in a spot where his brush was about to go. Jock stopped brushing and started looking.

"Another grandbaby, Dad."

Jock had tears in his eyes when he took one beefy arm, strong for a man of his years, and pulled her into his side.

"I need you to be happy for me," said Jessie.

"I am," Jock said gruffly.

"I need you to come to our party this weekend. Celebrate with us."

He nodded.

"Do you promise?"

He nodded again.

"I love you, Dad."

"I love you." Jock took the sonogram picture and tucked it into the front pocket of his shirt. "Now let me get back to work."

For now, it was enough. For her father, that was a giant step in the right direction.

"You're going to love Hawk one day, Dad."

Jock didn't look at her; he kept right on brushing the gelding. "Don't push it."

"Okay." She laughed, but said over her shoulder, "But you will."

Chapter Nine

Several days of working with Sugar Creek's herds had changed Hawk's outlook for the better. At his core, he was an Australian farmer, inextricably linked to the land of Daintree Downs. But he found that he was beginning to feel a deep connection with the land of Sugar Creek—the mountains, the clear creeks, the rich green grazing land. And since it didn't conflict with the outside work restrictions on his visa, he was able to drive and work on the ranch. He had the privilege of freedom that so many did not—freedom that had always driven him.

"I think this is the one." Hawk studied himself in the full-length mirror at Revolvr Menswear in downtown Bozeman.

The store clerk had selected a black suit with thin

pinstripes—the first time Hawk had seen himself in a suit in quite a while.

"I like it," Bruce agreed.

They had both taken the morning off from ranch work to go into town and find Hawk a suit for his upcoming wedding.

"How long for alterations?" Hawk asked the clerk.

"For the Brand family?" the man said. "I will have it ready in two weeks."

Hawk changed into his regular clothes; paid for the suit, shirt, belt and matching tie; and then headed toward their next destination: the local jewelry store.

"Bruce Brand!" a petite blond-haired woman exclaimed.

"Good to see you again, Tiffany," Bruce said.

"This is a surprise." Tiffany smiled at them. "I don't usually see you until the holidays."

"I'm not shopping for me," his future brother-in-law was quick to say. "We're here for him."

"And who might you be?" Tiffany turned her attention to Hawk.

He held out his hand. "Hawk Bowhill."

"Oh, my!" The jeweler's eyelashes fluttered quickly as she shook his hand. "That accent! *Très* sexy! What brings you in today?"

"I'm here to pick out some wedding bands."

"Wonderful," she said.

"And—" Hawk pulled a small bag out of his pocket, opened it, took the stone out and put it in his open palm for Tiffany to examine "—I need a setting for this."

Tiffany's eyes widened. "That is a magnificent black opal."

"It took me quite a while to find the right one."

"Well, you certainly succeeded," Tiffany said. "May I?"

Originally, Hawk had hoped to give Jessie his grandmother's engagement ring, but his grandfather refused when he found out that he was moving to Montana. It was then that he began a hunt for a black opal with orange, yellow, blue, green and—the most coveted color—red. It had taken him longer than he had wanted, but he had finally found a two-carat stone with as much fire and life as the woman he was about to marry.

Tiffany, who had taken the stone from his hand, looked up from it. "And who is the lucky lady?"

"I'm marrying Jessie."

"My sister," Bruce clarified.

"I surmised." Tiffany's eyes crinkled at the corners when she smiled. "We can find you a perfect setting for this. And depending on the budget, we could make a custom setting unique to this stone."

"That's what I want." Hawk nodded. "Custom."

All of the Brand men had purchased jewelry from Tiffany for one occasion or another. She was knowledgeable, thorough and took her time to find him the best set of wedding rings that would suit the specialness of the black opal engagement ring. During the design process, Tiffany asked pointed questions about accent diamonds, setting type and position of the main stone.

"Is this what you had in mind?" Tiffany held up a rough but gorgeous sketch of the possible custom setting.

"That's brilliant, yeah." Hawk nodded. "When can I pick it up?"

A look of concern flashed on Tiffany's face. "How soon do you need it?"

"I wanted to give it to her this weekend," he said, "before the gender-reveal party."

She shook her head while she thought.

"He's here on the K1 fiancé visa," Bruce added. "So everything is pretty rushed."

"I see." Tiffany tapped a long, red nail on the glass countertop. After several seconds of tapping, the jeweler said, "For the Brand family, I can make it happen."

Hawk paid the bill, thanked Tiffany, and then they headed toward Bruce's truck. Once inside the cab, Hawk said, "It pays to be a Brand around here."

Bruce laughed. "It has its perks, that's for sure. There are a lot of us, and we spend a lot of money in this town. Anywhere else we need to stop before we head back?"

"Where can I buy some white holiday lights?" Hawk asked. He had a plan in mind for his proposal.

"If you need Christmas lights, you don't need to buy them." Bruce backed out the parking space.

"Shayna, Noah's wife, has more Christmas lights than Santa Claus himself. She puts a Christmas display up every year that's pretty legendary in these parts. Let me give her a call and see if we can swing by."

"Well—" Shayna Brand looked around the barn after she flipped the switch to turn on the lights "—I think we've done our best here."

"Agreed." Savannah joined her sister-in-law in the center of the barn at Liam's cabin. "What do you think, Hawk? Have we captured your vision?"

Hawk wasn't certain that he'd had a "vision" before his soon-to-be sisters-in-law shared *their* vision for the space with him. He'd just wanted to put up some white lights to add ambience for the evening proposal he was planning for his beloved. While Jessie was spending some much-needed girl time with some of her closest childhood friends, he had been busy with Shayna and Savannah, turning the old barn into a romantic getaway perfect for presenting his fiancée with the custom ring he had designed with Tiffany.

"I think it's better than I had in mind," he said. "Thanks to you both."

Shayna had her hands resting on her large belly; she was in her final trimester with her first child with her husband, Noah.

"Everything is better with Christmas lights," Shayna said, following up with a joyful, tinkling laugh and a surprised look on her face. "My son just kicked me! I think he must be happy about the Christmas lights too."

"The summer of Brand babies," Savannah said, her hands naturally moving to her own growing baby bump.

"It seems to be a bit of an outbreak," Hawk noted.

"Well," Bruce's wife said, "with seven brothers, all married, plus Jessie, it's bound to happen. More the merrier, I think."

"Agreed," Shayna said before she gave Hawk and Savannah a goodbye hug.

"We'd better skedaddle and let you get ready for your big night," Savannah said. "You just shoot me a text when Jessie is on her way home, and I'll bring the food over."

Savannah, one of the best cooks in the family, had offered to make one of Jessie's favorite meals— homemade lasagna. According to his fiancée, Savannah's lasagna was legendary and second to none.

"I will." Hawk hugged both of them, and then he went back to setting up the barn.

He brought a small table and two chairs into the barn aisle. He had found the table and chairs in one of the storage sheds and then went back to the cabin to shower and shave. It was odd, but he was actually nervous. He'd already proposed, she had said yes and they had a baby on the way. It didn't make sense that he should be nervous, and yet he was.

To keep himself occupied, he walked down to the barn to double check the setup. Pleased, he returned to the cabin and sat down in one of the rocking chairs. He was still rocking away, working on settling his nerves, when Jessie called.

"Hello, love," he said, happy to hear her voice.

"Hello, yourself, handsome," she said playfully. "Miss me yet?"

"Absolutely."

"Should I come home early?"

Hawk's stomach knotted; his plan was dependent on surprising Jessie at dusk when the lights would provide the best effect.

"I'm going to be out with Bruce until six." He told a white lie in order to keep the surprise a surprise. "You're having a good time, aren't you?"

"Incredible," she said. "So much to catch up on. And your ears must be burning, because I've been bragging about you for hours."

"Is that what that was?" he joked with her. "Well, no need to stop now. I'll see you later. I love you."

"I love you!" she exclaimed.

"That makes me a very lucky man."

"Hey!" Jessie gave Hawk a hello hug and kiss. "I'm so sorry! I thought I would be home earlier."

"No worries," Hawk told her and he meant it. As it turned out, Jessie staying out later with her friends and getting home when it was dark out had allowed the display of white lights carefully strewn throughout the barn to have more impact.

"I have a surprise for you," Hawk said, holding a clean bandanna in his hand.

"You do." She smiled, her blue eyes bright with happiness. "What is it?"

"Do you trust me?"

"With my life."

"Then I'll need to blindfold you."

"Kinky," she said flirtatiously.

"That's for later," he bantered, tying the bandanna over her eyes.

Slowly and carefully, Hawk led her out the door, down the stairs and across the yard to the barn. Hawk flipped on the lights, amazed at how bright and sparkly they appeared. It looked like a room full of white diamonds, twinkling and winking in the night.

Hawk stood behind her. "Close your eyes."

"Okay. They're closed," she said.

He untied the blindfold and then wrapped his arms around her body from behind. "Now open them."

It took only a split second for her eyes to adjust and to get her bearings. With Hawk's strong arms wrapped around her, his sexy, spicy scent enveloping her, Jessie felt tears of surprise, joy and love well up.

"Hawk." She said his name, her eyes flitting all around the transformed barn.

"Do you like it?"

"It's the most romantic thing anyone has ever done for me." She turned in his arms, held on to him tightly and kissed him sweetly on the lips.

"That's what I was aiming for."

With her arm linked through his, they walked together into the barn.

"I had some help," he told her.

"Well, I know Shayna had to have been here. She's the queen of Christmas."

Hawk led her to the table and took the lasagna out of the bag that was keeping it warm.

"Is that Savannah's lasagna?" she asked, her stomach immediately growling at the first whiff of the dish.

"Yes, it is."

"Now I know why you told me to just get an appetizer with my friends!"

"Guilty." He smiled down at her. "And I have to confess. I wasn't with Bruce today."

"I can see that!" Jessie laughed. She loved this about Hawk. He was a masculine, tough, rugged man who was also incredibly romantic. It was a killer combination—the best of both worlds.

"Let's eat!" she said, making to sit down.

"Just one thing first." Hawk stopped her.

"One thing that can't wait?"

"One thing that can't wait," he said, pulling a ring box out of his pocket and kneeling down in front of her.

In that moment, she forgot all about the lasagna calling her name, and her entire focus was on the man she loved with every fiber of her being.

"Oh, Hawk." Her hand went to cover her mouth, and she felt those tears of joy rising again.

"I'm sorry this took so long..."

She shook her head no to reassure him. Their love was much more important, more rare and special, than any ring could ever represent.

"But, my gorgeous, incredible, Jess..." Hawk opened the top of the ring box to present the engagement ring. "Will you make me the happiest bloke on the planet? Will you be my wife?"

At first, Jessie was caught off guard by the ring nestled in the blue velvet of the box. The ring was gorgeous and Jessie could feel how much effort Hawk had put into the design. Of course, it still hurt that his grandfather would not allow Hawk to give her his grandmother's ring, but she didn't want to dwell on that disappointment now. Tonight was all about their love for each other.

"Of course I will," she finally said. "A thousand times, yes!"

Hawk stood up, took the exquisite ring, with the center stone a fiery black opal surrounded by diamonds, with more diamonds in the bezel set on the shank.

Jessie admired the ring, moving her finger so the white lights would bring out the life in the diamonds. "It's perfect, Hawk. I've never seen a more beautiful ring in my life."

Hawk held her hands, staring down at her with more love than she had ever seen on anyone's face. This man loved her in a way she had never known was possible; it was the stuff of fairy tales, and now it was her real life.

"I had this made especially for you." Hawk lifted her hand to kiss it. "I searched all of Australia to find the rarest of black opals."

She kissed him deeply, holding him just as tightly as he was holding her.

Hawk pulled out her chair and seated her before he took his own.

"I can't believe you planned all of this for me," she said, taking the plate he handed her, the aroma of cheese, sausage and Savannah's homemade seasoned tomato sauce tantalizing her senses.

"I love you," Hawk said simply.

"I know you do," she said, enjoying the feel of the weight of her new engagement ring on her finger. "And I love you."

Under the white lights, and with the sound of the horses whickering to each other in the nearby pasture, Jessie dined with her fiancé, laughing as they always did and making plans for their future. For Jessie, what meant the most was the fact that, for the first time since the first few days of his arrival in Montana, Hawk was wearing the Stetson she had bought for him. Perhaps it wasn't a big sign for most people, but for her, it was as bright as a Las Vegas casino sign. Hawk was signaling to her that he was embracing his life with her in Montana.

"Here's to you." She held out her wineglass filled

with sparkling grape juice. "For turning this night into one of the most memorable of my life."

"No." Hawk held out his bottle of beer. "Here's to us, my love. Here's to us."

Babies, as a general Brand family rule, weren't just a blessing—they were always a cause for major celebrations. Jock wanted to fill up Sugar Creek with generations of Brands in the hopes that the land would stay in the family into the next century. Within the last several years, her older brothers had added substantially to the clan. Shane and Rebecca had a perfect little girl named Harley; Colt and Lee had a baby boy who they had named Jock, but everyone called him Junior. Now, Shayna was quickly approaching her due date with a baby boy. Jessie and Savannah were next.

"I'm so excited!" Jessie said as they pulled up to Bruce and Rebecca's house for the joint gender-reveal party. "Are you?"

"I'm ready," Hawk said. "It's been a bloody long wait."

"What do you think of the name Fern for a girl?" She reached for his hand as they walked together toward the house.

"Absolutely not." Hawk frowned at her. "What about Artemis?"

"Were you dropped on your head as a baby?" She frowned back at him. "That's not just a *no*, it's a *hell no*!"

"You know—" he smiled down at her affectionately "—I used to think you were more open-minded and progressive. The name means 'virgin goddess of the moon.'"

"Virgin goddess? There is not a snowball's chance in Hades that I'm putting that kind of pressure on our daughter! Next!" She laughed, feeling lighthearted and giddy that they would soon know the gender of their baby.

"On second thought, that might be too much pressure for one baby girl."

"Ya think?" She bumped her hip to his right before they walked up the stairs to the front porch.

"When you're right, you're right, gorgeous."

Jessie opened the front door of the house. "We're here!"

With a huge smile on her face, Savannah met her in the foyer, hugged her and tugged her away from Hawk.

"The boys are out back," Savannah told Hawk.

Hawk gave Jessie a quick kiss and then headed toward the back of the house, only to be waylaid by Lee. "We haven't met yet, Hawk…"

"I'm so sorry, Lee!" Jessie said. "Hawk, this is Colt's wife, Lee. Lee, Hawk."

"It's nice to meet you." Hawk lifted his hat in a gentlemanly fashion.

"Welcome to the craziness," Lee said, her pretty face and kind eyes smiling in welcome. On her hip, a hefty toddler with chubby cheeks looked at Hawk with large round Brand blue eyes.

"And this little guy is Junior." Jessie tickled the boy's toes. "Just look at how handsome you are." To Lee, she said, "He's gotten so big."

"I know. He's growing like a weed," Lee responded, then turned to Hawk. "Would you mind taking Junior out to Colt? I've got to use two hands."

Hawk looked stunned, as if Lee had asked him to do something *shocking*. He didn't say a word and he didn't move.

"You'll be fine." Lee handed her chubby-cheeked son over to Hawk, who appeared to be very uncomfortable holding the boy, especially when Junior began to fuss and reach for his mother.

"You look like a natural." Jessie patted him on the shoulder.

"Where is Colt again?" Hawk had an odd expression on his face; it was a mixture of trepidation and naked fear.

"Right through that door." Lee pointed.

Together, Jessie and Lee watched Hawk book it toward the back door, obviously looking to hand off the toddler to his father.

"He has a long way to go," Lee said with a laugh. "But he will get there. They all do."

"Miles and miles," Jessie agreed. "Good thing he's a quick learner."

"A very good thing."

They returned to the kitchen to help Savannah

with the food prep. They had added two leaves to the dining room table; in the center of the table, two cakes, one for Savannah and one for Jessie, were beautifully made and ready to reveal the gender of their babies.

"The cakes are so pretty," Jessie said to Savannah. "I can't wait."

"I've been chomping at the bit too." Her sister-in-law smiled. "It's actually been harder than I thought."

"Agreed!"

Soon Lilly arrived, and Jessie was the first to greet her with a long hug.

"Oh, my darling girl," Lilly said. "I'm so happy to see you."

"Is Daddy coming?"

Lilly sent her a reassuring motherly smile. "Yes. He is. The sonogram picture won him over. That's my smart cookie."

Savannah and Lee greeted Lilly. Seeing her mother with her daughters-in-law made Jessie feel a twinge of jealousy that she wouldn't have her own mother-in-law to share memories with.

"Kate and Callie are almost here," Lee called out to the group.

"Has anyone heard from Hunter and Skyler?" Lilly asked, washing her hands at the kitchen sink.

Jessie nodded, chewing a piece of cheese from one of the plates. After she swallowed, she said, "Skyler is finishing a test online. They'll be heading over right after. Shane and Rebecca and their brood are also on their way."

"It's a full house!" Savannah exclaimed.

Lilly's phone rang and she stepped away from the kitchen. Gabe and Bonita, rarely available, passed Lilly on the way in the front door.

"Out back?" Gabe asked Lee, grabbing a few crackers from the tray.

"Out back," Lee said, hugging Bonita.

A couple of minutes later, Lilly came back in followed by Kate and Callie. Jessie was alarmed to see that Lilly's face was ashen and pinched, her joyful energy sapped.

"Is Liam with you?" Lilly asked Kate.

"No, Mom, he's not," Kate said. "He went to Three Forks on an emergency call."

"That's too far away!" Lilly exclaimed. "My sweet girl could be dead by the time he gets here!"

Chapter Ten

Hawk was grateful when Jessie came to get him. Jock Junior had thrown up on him, and now he smelled like curdled milk.

"What's wrong?" he asked her when the worried look on Jessie's lovely face turned his mind from the trivial to the serious.

"Mama's cow has gone into labor. She's two weeks late as it is. It doesn't look good."

All of the men on the back porch stood up immediately. Once inside, Colt handed his son to Lee as they joined the circle of family around Lilly.

"What's going on?" Colt asked.

"Josh just called," Lilly said of one of many barn managers. "Beauty started labor nearly an hour ago."

"Where is she?" Colt asked urgently.

"Out in the pasture behind the south barn," Lilly said. "But labor has stopped completely, and Josh thinks the calf is too big for the birth canal!"

Colt cursed. "Why didn't he call us the minute she went into labor?"

"We can litigate that later," Bruce interjected, a grim look on his face.

"I'm with Bruce. We need to get to her straight-away." In that moment, Hawk didn't feel like an outsider looking in—he was a cattleman at his core, and he had lived through countless emergencies at his cattle station.

"I'm coming," Bonita said firmly. "If I can resuscitate a human, I just might come in handy."

Gabe, the quiet one of Jessie's brothers, nodded his agreement on all counts. Colt led the way to the door, his car keys in his right hand. Hawk was part of the group, and no one asked him to stay behind. Maybe they just needed another set of hands; either way, it made him feel, for the first time, like he was part of this large tight-knit family.

At the door, Jessie put her hand on his arm. "You can save them, can't you?"

In his lifetime, he had assisted hundreds of cows in the birthing process. The conditions in the outback were brutal, much worse than most cows would face here in Montana. But each birth was unique, and he hadn't been able to save every calf.

"You know I'll try."

Lilly followed her sons out onto the porch.

"Mama," Jessie called out to her mother. "They will do everything in their power to save them both. But just in case they can't..."

"I need to be with her," Lilly said firmly. "She knows me. I can keep her calm. And if she—" Lilly paused and swallowed back tears "—if she dies, she will die with me by her side."

"If you can keep her calm," Hawk said, "we need you."

At what he took as faith in his judgment, Jessie nodded her head without another word, kissed him quickly and then watched from the doorway as they loaded into two trucks.

From the porch, she hollered to him, "Call me as soon as you can!"

Hawk gave her a thumbs-up to let her know that he had heard her. This wasn't what any of them had expected when they started the day anticipating a family get-together to celebrate adding new members to the Brand family. But as Hawk knew well from his life on Daintree Downs, he had to plan for the best but expect the worst. The animals took precedence over everything.

"How long until we get there?" Hawk asked Colt as he reached for the handle to keep his body steady when they caught some air from flying over bumps on the back road.

"Ten minutes max."

"God help us," Lilly said from the back seat. "Please keep my sweet girl safe."

Hawk forced himself from saying anything that would upset Lilly more. But experience had taught him that unfortunately, time wasn't on their side. When a calf was stuck in the birth canal, every second mattered. He'd do everything he could.

When they arrived on the scene, Josh was kneeling beside Beauty, who was lying on her side. Their group jumped out of the vehicle to run over to the distressed cow.

"It's breech!" Josh was drenched in sweat, and his clothes were soaked with blood and amniotic fluid. "I managed to break the sac, but I can't find the second foot!"

Lilly went down on her knees near Beauty's head; the cow's eyes were shut, her breathing labored, and she was groaning.

"Hang in there, sweet girl," Lilly said, petting the cow's large head. "We're going to help you."

Hawk didn't hesitate—he just acted on instinct. He grabbed a long plastic glove from the small pile of supplies Josh had brought with him, squeezed lube on the glove and then dropped down near Beauty's hind end.

"I couldn't find that foot," Josh said, his voice weak and wavering. "I just couldn't *find* it."

Hawk slid his arm carefully into the birth canal and began the process of feeling for the calf's hooves.

"The leg is bent all the way forward," he told the

group, closing his eyes so he could block out the others and use the experienced senses of his fingers.

"There's one hoof," he said, slipping his arm in farther to find the second hoof.

"If we don't get the calf out soon, it's as good as dead," Gabe said somberly.

Lilly leaned her head forward, tears streaming down her face now as she whispered to her beloved cow, "Don't give up. You're so strong. I believe in you."

Hawk continued to search until he felt the second hoof trapped up near the calf's head. "And there's the second."

A hopeful cheer burst out among the small group.

"Can you bring it forward?" Bruce asked.

"I'm working on it." He kept his eyes closed and slowly, carefully began the painstaking chore of moving the second hoof down to the birth canal.

"Get the rope," he heard Gabe say. "If he can get that hoof in position, it's going to take all of us pulling to get it out."

"She's not pushing!" Lilly exclaimed. "Why isn't she pushing?"

"She's tuckered out." Josh's voice was thick with guilt. "God only knows how long she'd been at this before I found her. How in tarnation she broke out of her birthing stall, I'll never know."

Hawk was grateful that the chattering stopped. They were far from out of the woods, and time was not on their side. They could still lose both the mother and the calf.

"Gotcha!" Hawk let out his breath, feeling the sting of beads of sweat rolling into his eyes when he opened them.

"We have two hooves, Lilly!" Bonita called out the news in the steady voice of a woman who had seen many emergencies in her life as a doctor.

"Where's the bloody rope?" Hawk yelled, not ready to celebrate.

"Here." Bruce appeared next to him.

Without bothering to waste a second of energy thanking Bruce for the rope, Hawk continued to focus on Beauty. He had to sweep images flashing in his mind of the calves and heifers he had lost along the way while he tied the rope around both of the calf's ankles just above the tiny hooves.

Jessie's brothers stacked their hands next to his on the rope, and together they began to pull. Beauty lifted her head up with a groan.

"I just got a contraction." Bonita was positioned at Beauty's back, her hands on the cow's distended stomach.

"That's right, Beauty!" Lilly said urgently. "Push!"

With each contraction, the men pulled on the rope. Slowly, the calf's legs began to emerge.

"Come on, Beauty!" Hawk yelled, his hands burning from the grip he had on the rope.

After nearly thirty minutes of pulling, Beauty had

one long, hard contraction, and the wet floppy calf slipped out of the birth canal and into the world. The calf blinked once at them, its tongue hanging out of its mouth.

"It's alive!" Bruce shouted to his mother. "And it's a boy!"

The calf kicked twice, took one short breath and then didn't take another. The calf's body went limp in their collective arms.

"Bonnie!" Gabe shouted to his wife. "It stopped breathing."

"Move!" Bonita leapt into action. "Everyone, move!"

The men backed up quickly and let the doctor do her best to revive the calf. Bonita cleared out the fluid from the calf's throat, plugged the nostril and held its mouth shut. "When I tell you to push on its chest, Gabe, you damn well better push."

"Yes, ma'am." Gabe followed the direction.

There were many tense minutes while Bonita blew air into the calf's nostril and then signaled for Gabe to compress the chest.

Lilly had her eyes closed, her head tilted back, with Beauty's head resting in her lap as she whispered prayers up to the sky.

For Hawk, it seemed like a lifetime waiting helpless while Bonita and Gabe provided CPR to the calf. Finally, Bonita sat back on her heels, her face red from exertion, tears of joy in her eyes.

"He's breathing," Bonnie said in a weak, gravelly

voice with tears flowing freely down her cheeks onto the bloody material of her shirt and jeans. "Let's get him to his mother."

All of the men joined in the effort to help move the calf over to where Beauty could smell her newborn and hopefully begin to clean it.

"Oh, Beauty!" Lilly was openly crying. "Look what you made? He's the most handsome boy I've ever seen!"

After a few minutes of the mother not acknowledging her calf, Beauty rolled up onto her front legs, sniffed the calf and then began to lick her newborn.

"Oh, thank the Lord." Josh closed his eyes for a moment prayer before he said to Lilly, "I wouldn't have been able to face you if they'd died on my watch, Mrs. Brand. I swear I did everything I could."

Lilly, Hawk had begun to notice, was a sweet, forgiving woman. Admirable.

"You saved them." Lilly reached for Josh's hand. "You called us and that saved them. Thank you."

Josh ducked his head; Hawk could tell the man would have many sleepless nights wondering what he could have done differently. But having the forgiveness of the matriarch of the family should go a long way to soothe the man's guilt.

"What are you going to name him, Lilly?" Bonita had been keeping a keen, watchful eye on the calf to ensure that it kept right on breathing.

"That's an easy one." Lilly's face was alight with happiness. "Lucky Boy."

* * *

After they saved Lucky, they all waited until Beauty was on her feet before they managed to get both mom and baby back into the barn and into a clean stall of fresh hay. From beginning to end, the task had taken them hours, and everyone was exhausted and covered in blood, sweat, dirt, mud and amniotic fluid.

"We're going to have to postpone the reveal," Jessie told Savannah on the phone.

"I figured as much," her sister-in-law said. "Maybe tomorrow."

"Tomorrow for sure."

On a family text chain, everyone confirmed that they could attend the gender reveal the following day—even Noah and Shayna. Shayna was nine months along in her pregnancy, her due date was just around the corner, and everyone was excited to welcome another Brand baby into the ever-growing brood.

When they pulled up to Bruce and Savannah's home and they all piled out, Lilly made a beeline to Hawk.

"I am so grateful to you, Hawk," Lilly said. "What you bring to the table as an outback cattleman is invaluable. We have a lot to learn from you, son."

"Thank you, Mrs. Brand."

Lilly raised an eyebrow at him and gave him an expression that reminded him of her earlier request.

"Thank you, Lilly."

Hawk's mind was still reeling when they got into the Jeep. Jessie had told him long ago that it was Lilly, not Jock, who was the silent leader of the family. And now Lilly had just given him the greatest stamp of approval.

"I was so proud of you today," Jessie said. "Everyone got to see just how amazing you are."

"I would have been gutted if we lost that calf," Hawk said.

Jessie put her hand on his arm. "I know. Me too. But you saved him, Hawk."

"It took all of us."

"Yes, it did," Jessie agreed. "But in my mom's eyes, you're the hero of the day."

Hawk smiled at that. "Your mom called me *son*."

"I *know*! You couldn't get a better stamp of approval than that." Jessie smiled. "You saved Beauty *and* Lucky. For mom, they aren't just cows—they are her children."

"I was just grateful that it turned out like it did. It's not always the case," Hawk said. Every calf or heifer that he had lost was permanently burned in his memory.

"Me too."

"Now, if your dad could just give me a break."

"Trust me." Jessie had a ring of assuredness in her voice. "If *Mom* gives her stamp of approval, which is exactly what she did today, then it's only a matter of time before Dad comes around."

"I hope you're right." Hawk pulled up to Liam's cabin and shifted into Park.

"I am," she said. "One hundred percent."

Together they climbed up the porch stairs and stripped out of their clothes. Jessie stripped out of her underwear and stood naked before him. The changes in her body—the full breasts and her beautiful rounded belly—made all of the blood rush to his groin. His eyes swept the full length of his fiancée's body before he stripped out of his underwear so his bride-to-be could see just how sexy she was to him.

Without a word, Jessie reached for his hand and led him to the bathroom. After the hot, steamy water cleansed their bodies of the day's hard work, they fell into bed with bodies intertwined and made love until they were both exhausted.

"I love you so much," Jessie said languidly.

"I love you." Hawk had his hand on her belly.

After a few moments of silence, Hawk moved his hand up to one of Jessie's breasts and began to massage it.

"Mmm." Jessie's made a pleasurable noise, her eyes still closed. "That feels so good."

The pleasurable little sounds Jessie was making managed to arouse him again. Hawk closed his eyes, grit his teeth and buried his face in Jessie's neck. He'd already made love to her twice, and now here he was ready for a third.

"You need me," she said.

"Give me a minute, it'll go away."

Jessie tugged on his arm, pulling him toward her. "You need me."

"Are you sure?" he asked, his body taut with anticipation.

Hawk moved between her lovely thighs and slipped into her warmth. He drew her nipple into his mouth, suckling as he moved inside her.

"Yes, my beauty," Hawk murmured against her breast as he felt her quicken.

When he had her panting and moaning and squirming beneath him, Hawk allowed himself to let go and ride that same wave of ecstasy with his beloved. And after they came down from the clouds, Jessie turned onto her side, Hawk wrapped himself around her, his hand on her growing baby belly, and they both fell asleep with a new sense of hope that the Jock Brand would finally approve of their marriage and that they would be able to plan their wedding without fear that their special day wouldn't turn into a family feud.

"My love?" Hawk said after a several moments of silence.

"Hmm?" his fiancée murmured groggily. Her breathing was regular and her eyes closed; Hawk knew that she was half asleep, but he still felt compelled to ask her something that had been in his heart for a long time.

"If we have a girl, I would like to name her after my grandmother and my great-aunt."

Jessie turned a bit in his arms; she opened her eyes and looked up at his face through half-open eyes. "You've never mentioned this before."

"I know." He nodded. "I know. But lately, I just can't get the idea out of my mind. They were both such strong, capable women. Kindhearted, motherly, but with spines of steal."

Her eyes more open now, Jessie seemed to be mulling over his request. After some thought, she said, "Your grandmother's name was Debra?"

He nodded. "And my great-aunt's name was Yvonne. They both had a major hand in raising me after my parents died. My grandfather taught me cattle, but my grandmother and great-aunt taught me how to be a good man."

Jessie spun completely around in his arms so she was facing him; she put a hand on his cheek sweetly. "You are such a good man. Such a loving, strong man."

"Thank you." He took her hand in his and kissed it.

"If we *are* having a girl," she said, her eyes looking deeply into his, "her name will be Debra Yvonne Bowhill."

The next day the family gathered for the joint gender-reveal party at Savannah and Bruce's. The house was crackling with excitement and anticipation. Unfortunately, Gabe and his wife, Bonita, couldn't attend, and Hunter attended without his wife, Skyler.

"Is everything okay?" Jessie asked Hunter under her breath. The two of them were more connected than just about any of her brothers. They had deliberately chosen adjacent homesteads on Sugar Creek so that they could raise their families together side by side.

"She's just tired," Hunter said, and Jessie felt that he was being a bit coy but decided not to dig deeper. This was a day for celebration, a day to celebrate new life coming into the Brand family. Hunter would share if he needed to in due time.

"You know I'm always here for you, right?" She hugged Hunter.

"You bet I do." He kissed her on the top of her head and gave her a quick squeeze in return.

"Okay," she said. "Just so you know."

On the way to the kitchen, Jessie overheard Liam say, "I tell you Pop, I couldn't have done a better job than Hawk. He did everything right; if he had hesitated for a minute, the calf would've been dead, and Beauty might have been right behind him."

"Is there anything I can do to help?" Jessie asked Savannah, who was fluttering around the kitchen, her auburn hair swept up into a high ponytail and her the fair freckled skin of her face flushed prettily.

"It's time!" Savannah said. "Are you ready?"

"Am I going first?"

"Yes," her sister-in-law said, lifting the cake off the kitchen counter. "Will you gather everyone at the dining table?"

Jessie heard the nervous excitement in her own voice as she went from room to room, porch to porch, to let everyone in the family know that it was time! On the way back to the dining room, Jessie grabbed Hawk's hand, and together they rushed to the table.

"Is everyone here?" Jessie looked around the table at all of the expectant faces. The children were squirming and wiggling and eventually ended up under the table.

Savannah nodded as she handed a cutting knife to Hawk. Together, with both hands on the knife, they sliced into the cake and then pulled the first piece out. Inside, the cake was colored a very bright shade of pink.

"It's a girl!" Hawk exclaimed as he pulled her into his arms. "We're having a girl!"

"You wanted a girl." Jessie hugged him back, loving the sound of her family cheering for them.

"I wanted a girl." Hawk looked down into her face. "I wanted a girl just like you."

"Do you have a name?" Several family members called out the question.

Jessie smiled brightly around the table, her arm around Hawk's as his was around her. "Debra Yvonne Bowhill."

"After my grandmother and great-aunt."

After the family toasted Debra Yvonne, it was Savannah and Bruce's turn. They cut the cake and revealed the bright blue color.

"A boy!" everyone exclaimed. Bruce picked up his daughter and held her with one arm while the other encircled his wife's shoulders.

"Name?" several people called out in unison.

Savannah looked up at her husband, and he gave her the nod. Her hand on her growing belly, Savannah said, "His name is Isaiah Brand."

Jessie wasn't surprised by Savannah's choice. It was a strong biblical name, and Savannah was very connected to her church and her relationship with God.

The family raised their glasses for Isaiah Brand, welcoming him into the family. Jessie noticed that Savannah slipped away for a moment, and when she returned, she had another cake in her hands. With a secretive pleased smile on her face, Savannah scanned the surprised expressions on the faces of the family.

"Wait a minute!" Jessie blurted out. "Is someone else pregnant here or are you having—"

"Twins!" Savannah finished for her. "We're having twins!"

Together, along with their daughter, Bruce and Savannah cut the second cake to reveal the same bright blue of their first cake.

"It's another boy!" the Brands exclaimed in unison before they started to clamor for a name.

"Quintin," Bruce said, "Quintin Brand."

"Here's to Debra Yvonne Bowhill, and Isaiah and Quintin Brand!" Jock held up his glass for a toast. For the briefest of moments, but long enough for her father to convey his message, Jock caught Hawk's eye the moment he said, "Welcome to the family!"

The sound of everyone gathered in a small space was loud and boisterous and full of laughter. Above that din, Jessie heard Shayna cry out and double over. The family quieted while Noah attempted to ascertain the problem. Their daughter, Isabella, who had been under the table, appeared and went to her stepmother's side.

"My water just broke!" Shayna said in a breathy voice, her hand on her very round stomach. "I think that Sawyer didn't want to miss all the fun."

"It's time?" Noah, a Marine, looked completely stunned. Although he was a father already, this would be his first time in the delivery room.

"Yes—" Shayna reached for her husband's arm as she stood upright "—it's time. Sawyer Brand is ready to meet the world."

As if they were a wave upon which they were riding, the entire family shuttled Shayna, Noah and Isabella to their vehicle, got them situated and on their way to the hospital.

"We'll meet you there!" Jessie yelled to her family from behind the wheel of her Jeep.

"See you there!"

"Are there always so many babies being born in your family?" Hawk asked as he buckled himself in.

"Always!" Jessie laughed happily. "We Brands love our babies!"

Chapter Eleven

The day after the gender-reveal party—and the day that Sawyer Brand decided it was time for him to make an appearance—Jessie wanted to retreat from the high energy of her family to spend some quiet one-on-one time with her fiancé. Despite his gradual acclimation to the entirely new world, she knew that Montana, Sugar Creek and the entire Brand family were overwhelming for Hawk. He was used to a very different life, where he spent days alone with his cattle camping under the stars.

"What about here?" Jessie asked.

"It's perfect." Hawk smiled at her.

They had decided a picnic at their stake on Sugar Creek was needed. It was a place where they could dream about their future home and imagine their baby girl growing up, healthy, happy and surrounded by a big family full of love for her.

Under the bows of an ancient oak tree and close enough to the creek to benefit from the cool breeze and soothing sound of the water dancing over the boulders, Hawk spread out a blanket for them.

"What did you pack for us?" He leaned on his side, propped up and, as he often did, admired her with his eyes full of love.

"Roast beef sandwiches." She unloaded some of the food from the picnic basket she had borrowed from Savannah. "Homemade root beer." Jessie handed him a thermos that was keeping the beverage cool.

Hawk sat upright, opened the lid and took a long draw of root beer. "This is bloody delicious."

Jessie nodded her head, busily unwrapping a hoagie for Hawk. She handed him a hoagie filled with roast beef slices and his favorite fixings. While she unwrapped her sandwich, Hawk took a giant bite of his and chewed happily. After he swallowed his first bite, he winked at her. "And this is bloody delicious too."

"I'm glad you're enjoying it."

Hawk made short work of the hoagie, so she pulled out another for him.

"I love you to bits. Do you know that?" he asked.

"Yes." She laughed and then teased him. "I do. But I hope it's for more important reasons than I knew to pack you a second sandwich."

"I don't know, love." Hawk prepared to devour the second hoagie. "This ticks a pretty important box for me."

They laughed and talked and enjoyed the tranquility of the scenery. But behind the smiles and laughter, Jessie sensed that there was something Hawk wasn't saying. Something he was holding back.

"It's peaceful here, isn't it?" she asked, studying her fiancé's profile.

"It is that." Hawk tossed his empty hoagie wrapping into the basket.

"Can you see yourself here?" she probed. "Forever?"

"The only thing I can see myself doing *forever* is love you." He reached for her hand, drew it close and then kissed it.

It was a dodge; she knew it and she had to consider if she was going to keep digging and possibly ruin the moment or drop it and just enjoy herself.

"I like that spot right over there." Hawk nodded to a large fallen log they had sat on the first time she had shown him the property. "It's one of my favorites."

"Then let's go over there and enjoy it together."

They cleaned up any remaining napkins and food and put them securely in the basket before walking hand in hand, arms swinging playfully, over to the fallen log. The log offered a nice place to sit and enjoy the scenery.

On the short trek to the creek, Jessie asked, "Did

you tell your grandfather that we're having a girl? And that we're naming her after his wife?"

A dark cloud quickly drifted across Hawk's face. If she didn't know him as well as she did, she would have missed it entirely.

"I gave him a call, but he didn't answer."

"He didn't answer?"

"No." Hawk tried, but failed, to keep the hurt out of his voice. "He didn't."

Jessie sat down, but now she felt like a bloodhound that just found a scent and was determined to track it down. Every time she had asked Hawk about his relationship with his grandfather, he always gave her the same song and dance about how things would shake out between them eventually.

Her stomach twisted into an uncomfortable knot; there *was* something he hadn't been telling her. Of course, she knew his grandfather was upset about the move to the US, which was to be expected. But for his grandfather not to take his call? That was entirely new information.

"Have you spoken to him at all since you've moved here?" she asked, more boldly and directly than was typical for her. Hawk didn't do well with too much prodding and digging; if she had pushed for answers, her fiancé was entirely capable of shutting down.

"Yes," he said, sitting down next to her.

When he didn't continue, she prodded him. "And?"

Hawk took her hand in his. "And he's angry."

"Of course." She nodded. "And?"

"And nothing." Frustration began to creep into Hawk's voice. "Let's not ruin this moment worrying about my grandfather, sweetheart. It'll all work itself out eventually."

"Do you really think so?"

"Yes." He kissed the hand he had been holding. "I do."

"Okay," Jessie said, resting her head on his shoulder. She didn't believe him entirely, but she *wanted* to believe him. Desperately.

They sat in silence, enjoying the sound of the creek water bubbling and gurgling as it wound its way around the larger boulders.

"This is my favorite spot on Sugar Creek," Hawk said.

"I'm glad."

"I can see Debra playing in this creek."

She linked her arm with his and snuggled closer to him, her mind imagining a little version of Hawk and herself, a daughter, splashing in the cold creek water.

"Do you really think that you can feel at home here?" She almost didn't get the question out of her mouth, and she steeled herself to hear the answer.

Hawk unhooked his arm from hers to put it around her shoulders so he could draw her closer still. "My home is where you are. My home is where my daughter is."

"I'm serious, Hawk."

"So am I," he said. "Of course I miss Daintree

Downs. That land is in my heart. It's in my DNA. But it's not home if you aren't there. Wherever you *are*, that's home."

Jessie was starting to feel emotional to the point of tears. Was she doing the right thing by wanting Hawk to live in Montana with her family?

"We can always spend summers in Australia," she said, her voice wavering a bit.

"Of course we can." He turned toward her so he could look into her eyes. "My beautiful Jessie, I want you to stop worrying about that and focus on having a healthy baby. That's what matters to me more than anything in this world. Your health. Our baby's health. Of course I miss Australia, but I'm not gutted about it. If I lost *you*, if I lost *Debra*, that would gut me entirely." He raised her chin gently with his finger. "Okay?"

She nodded, feeling better for having this talk. She scooted closer to him and rested her head on his shoulder.

"Debra will have so many people around to love her."

Hawk rested his chin on her head. "I see that now."

"She'll have cousins her own age living right on this land with her."

"Savannah and Bruce's twins and Sawyer," he agreed.

"She'll be the only girl in that age group."

"A little princess."

"A tomboy princess cowgirl," Jessie said.

"What could be better?"

"Nothing." Jessie sighed contentedly. "Absolutely nothing."

After spending time listening to soothing sounds of the creek, Hawk and Jessie returned to their picnic site, laying down in each other's arms to enjoy the sun.

Jessie turned into her fiancé's body and rested her head on his chest.

"You know…" Jessie said suggestively, "this is virgin land."

Jessie lifted up his head a bit so he could look into her face. "Are you suggesting that we christen this spot?"

"If you're up for it."

"My beautiful love, I am *always* up for it."

They were halfway undressed when the sound of a chainsaw shattered the peace and put a huge damper on their sexy moment.

"Who in the blazes is that?" Hawk asked, annoyed.

Jessie sat up and listened. "I think it's coming from Hunter's stake. It's right next door."

"Lousy bloody timing," Hawk complained.

"To be continued." Jessie fixed her clothing and stood up.

"To be continued," he agreed.

They cleaned up their picnic and headed back to the Jeep. They drove to the fork in the road, and Jessie asked him to follow the rocky, overgrown road up to Oak Tree Hill, the spot where Hunter and his wife, Skyler, intended to build their dream home one day.

"It is Hunter," Jessie said as they drove up the hill that was covered with ancient oak trees. "What in the world is he doing?"

Hawk put on the brakes, and she jumped out of the Jeep before he had shifted to Park. She ran up the hill, feeling the baby belly making it more difficult as she waved her arms and yelled, "Hunter! What are you doing? Stop!"

Her older brother, who was not even a year older than her, was taking an industrial chainsaw to one of the glorious old trees on the top of the hill.

"Hunter!" she yelled at him again. "Stop!"

Hunter was sweating through his shirt, and his face was smudged with grease. He looked like a hot mess, and he was so focused on trying to cut down one of his beloved oak trees that he didn't hear her yelling. She had to move into his line of sight to get his attention.

"Hunter!" she shouted. "Stop this!"

Hunter yanked the chainsaw out of the gash he had just created in the tree trunk, turned off the chainsaw and threw it onto the ground near his feet. Hunter's eyes, so like her own, had a crazed look in them.

"What are you doing out here?" Hunter snapped at her.

Hawk had just joined them, and she hoped he

would keep his mouth shut and not try to defend her, which would absolutely be his first inclination.

"What are you doing out here, Hunter?" She had her hands on her hips. "What are you doing to this tree? It's perfectly healthy! What did it do to deserve you cutting into it like that?"

Hunter rubbed his hands over his face several times and kicked the chainsaw with his boot.

"I'm letting off some steam," he finally said, looking saner, more connected, in his eyes.

All three of them stood in silence for several moments.

Finally, Jessie broke the silence. "Why? What's wrong?"

Hunter's eyes had tears in them; he brushed them away. And that's when it hit her—the only thing that could make even-keeled, salt-of-the-earth Hunter go mad would be Skyler, his beloved wife. His wife— who had been so sick, then so well.

"Oh, Hunter," Jessie said. "No."

She could tell that Hunter wasn't ready to be physically comforted, so she didn't try. "When did you find out?"

"Today."

"I'm so sorry."

Hunter looked off into the distance. "So am I."

When Hunter had first met Skyler, she was her father's guest on the ranch, and Hunter was assigned to be her guide. At first Hunter couldn't stand the idea of a city girl playing cowgirl on their working ranch. But once he met Skyler, a survivor of a rare lung cancer, Hunter fell in love with her spirit, her strength and her determination.

"What now?"

Hunter leaned back against the tree that he had just tried to fell. "She's booked on a flight back to New York. Her team is there. Her dad is there."

"And you?"

"I'll be leaving in two weeks. I need time to get things situated at the farm, make sure things are covered while we're away."

Hunter had purchased his best friend's family farm, which was just down the road from Sugar Creek, so Skyler would have a place to settle while she was taking college courses and deciding on the house they would eventually build on Oak Tree Hill.

"I can help. In any way I can," said Jessie.

"Thank you," Hunter said.

"That goes for me too, mate," Hawk said, after having been very quiet.

"I appreciate that," her brother said. "I really do."

Jessie walked over to Hunter and wrapped her arms around him. He had cooled off enough to accept this form of comfort from her.

"She's a fighter, Hunter. She'll beat it back a second time."

Hunter held on to her for a second longer before he stepped back. "She's tiny but mighty."

"Yes, she is," Jessie agreed. "And if she knew you were taking out your anger on one of her beloved trees, she'd kick your butt just as sure as she's going to kick cancer's butt."

That truth made Hunter flash a quick smile through his pain. "You're right about that."

"I know I am," Jessie said. "Now let's go over to your place so Hawk and I can see what you need done."

"Are you sure?"

"Hunter?" She looked at him like he had lost his ever-loving mind. "Don't be an idiot."

Hunter picked up his chainsaw and walked it over to his truck. "That's not always easy for me."

"I know," Jessie bantered back. "But Skyler and I still have a lot of hope for you."

Two weeks after Hawk had given her a custom-made engagement ring, Jessie gathered with all of the Brand women, along with Tony's mother, to support Callie during her final fitting of her wedding dress.

"Are you ready?" Callie called out from behind the fitting room curtain.

"Ready!" they all called out enthusiastically.

Callie had a very large entourage of people crammed onto kidney-shaped benches covered in silk and decorated prettily with flowers. All of the Brand wives made time in their schedules—even Skyler was attending virtually from her father's

New York home. So, with seven wives, Lilly, Tony's mother and Jessie, that brought the total entourage number to a staggering ten.

"Okay!" Callie said excitedly. "Here I come!"

The curtain was pulled back to reveal Callie in her bright white wedding dress.

Kate, her mother, stood up, her face so full of joy for her daughter. "Oh, Callie! You look absolutely beautiful!"

"Like a p-princess?" Callie stepped up on the raised platform with the help of the seamstress who had been working on the ball gown.

"Today, Callie," Kate said honestly, "you are a queen."

Callie looked at herself in the mirror, and she covered her mouth with her hands, her blue eyes sparkling with joy. "A queen."

The entourage gathered around Callie and Kate, giving them all the love and support they needed for this momentous occasion. Not since Liam had officially adopted Callie had Jessie seen Kate so undeniably happy and emotional.

"You are the most beautiful bride I have ever seen," Skyler said when Jessie brought her phone closer so her sister-in-law could see Callie.

Callie giggled behind her hand. "Thank you. I b-bet Tony will cry."

Tony's mom was wiping her eyes with a tissue. "I don't think there's any doubt about that."

Callie twirled around on the pedestal while a sale's clerk brought her crystal tiara and veil into the room. Once she was completely decked out in her bridal regalia, Callie turned back to her reflection in the mirror, then bent forward with her hands covering her mouth.

"I'm a b-bride, Mom," Callie said. "I'm a b-bride!"

Kate joined her daughter on the pedestal and wrapped her up in her arms. "You are, my wonderful daughter. You are a bride."

When Jessie hung up the video call with Skyler, and after they had all waited for Callie to get out of her wedding dress, her niece shocked her by saying, "Now, you should find a d-dress."

"No, Callie," Jessie said quickly. "This is your day."

"If it's my d-day, then I can say it's your d-day too," Callie said in her sweet, charming way, her hands on her hips in a determined-to-get-her-way pose.

After much coaxing and convincing, Jessie agreed to try on a couple of dresses, but only if Callie would pick them out. And much to her surprise, Callie picked out a flowing bohemian inspired dress, sparingly sprinkled with crystals, an illusion neck and sleeves, and an empire waist that floated over her growing belly.

"I can't believe it." Jessie stared at her reflection. "I always hear on those shows that brides will know when they have found their dress."

Callie was beaming at her. "Are you going to say y-yes to the d-dress?"

Jessie hugged her niece. "Yes, I can't believe it, but I am going to say yes to this dress. It's perfect."

Jessie returned to Hunter's farm feeling like she had springs on her feet. Her steps were light, with a happy mood to match. They had moved from Liam's cabin to Hunter's one hundred-year-old rehabbed whitewashed farmhouse with a wraparound porch and a wonderful front porch swing. Liam's cabin had served them well, but it did feel a bit too close to her family at the moment. On Hunter's farm, they were close but not *too* close. Hawk was thrilled and threw himself into farm work. It was the happiest she had seen him in Montana.

She opened the front door of the farmhouse, and she was about to call out Hawk's name when she heard his voice, angry, frustrated and upset, coming from the small office off the kitchen.

"Athena!" he said in a razor-sharp tone. "I fail to see why any of this is your business."

Jessie paused in the kitchen, her heart beating so hard in her chest. Athena was his grandfather's assistant turned lover after Hawk's grandmother had died. Hawk, thinking he was alone, had the phone on speaker.

"It is my business!" Athena yelled at him. "I'm his wife."

"No, you're not."

"Well, maybe I'm *not*," Athena said in a seething tone, "but at least me and my boy have stuck to him like glue and picked up the bloody pieces after you left! You'll be the death of him, I swear you will, you ungrateful son of a bitch!"

Chapter Twelve

Disbelieving what she had just overheard, Jessie raced to the small office, her heart feeling like it was up in her throat.

"Hawk?" She touched his shoulder. "What in the world was that all about? What's wrong?"

Wordlessly, Hawk wrapped her in his arms and rested his head on her belly.

"It's Grandpa," Hawk said in a rough, emotional voice. "He's had a stroke."

"Oh, no," she said, not wanting it to be true. Then she asked the question she was afraid to have answered. "Is he going to be okay?"

Hawk shook his head. "I don't know. I just don't know."

Jessie knelt down beside Hawk's chair. "I'm so

sorry, Hawk. I know things have been strained between you, and it's my fault."

"No, it's not," Hawk was quick to say. "It was my decision to move to Montana."

That wasn't quite right. Jessie knew how much pressure she had put on him in her quest to win regarding making Montana their home.

"Maybe I should take a quick trip back home to see him. He's the last of my family on my father's side."

Jessie froze for a second or two, the only thing seeming to move was her rapidly beating heart. Then she felt sick to her stomach.

"You can't," she said, her voice wavering. "We haven't gotten married yet. If you leave now, you may not be able to come back. You could miss the birth of our baby!"

Hawk stared off into the distance, but his eyes didn't seem to be focusing on anything in particular. "That's not an option," he finally said.

Jessie was both relieved to hear him say that and riddled with guilt at the same time. It was in this moment that she was acutely aware of the level of sacrifice Hawk had made in order to be with her and their child.

"We need to call our immigration lawyer," Jessie said. "There has to be a way we can work this out, Hawk. It's not fair that you have to choose between your grandfather and us. There has to be a way to fix this. There *must* be."

* * *

Two weeks after Hawk's combative phone call with Athena, he received news via text from her that his grandfather was out of the hospital and recuperating at home. Unfortunately, Hawk couldn't leave the country until he was married if he had any hope of returning, so he had to reach out remotely. No matter how often he tried to call him, his grandfather refused to pick up. But now, after having talked to Athena, he wasn't entirely sure that his grandfather even knew he was calling. Athena had mentioned her son, Gavin, on their last phone call. Hawk had grown up with Gavin—they were close to the same age and had both started as jackeroos, cowhands on Daintree Downs. But they weren't close. Hawk had seen, on multiple occasions, Gavin cutting corners or embellishing the truth. Hawk had always wondered why his grandfather didn't see the truth about Athena and Gavin. Where they were concerned, his grandfather always wore rose-colored glasses.

"How are they?" It was Jock. Hawk was deep in his own thoughts and hadn't heard anyone pull up to the barn where Lilly's belted Galloways were bedded down.

"I just gave them fresh water and hay," Hawk said. "I like to come and check on them."

Sometimes Hawk would come to visit the cows he had helped save; for whatever reason, they lifted his spirits when he was down or feeling homesick. Perhaps it was because they were a tangible success.

They were alive, healthy and happy, and he and the Brands had accomplished that together.

"Good to hear." Jock was wearing threadbare overalls, a dusty cowboy hat and old cowboy boots caked with mud. To look at him, a person wouldn't suspect that he was a multimillionaire.

Even though things had smoothed over a bit since their first meeting in Jock's office, Jessie's father still hadn't embraced him or given them his blessing.

Jock cleared his throat and said, "I haven't had a chance to thank you for what you did for Lilly."

Hawk turned his head toward the older man.

"Thank you."

"You're welcome," Hawk said, surprised. "I was happy to help."

"From what I've heard, you did a heck of a lot more than just help," Jock said. "You saved them, sure as I'm standing here."

After those words were spoken, they both fell silent again. Hawk wasn't sure, but it felt like perhaps Jock was trying to make an effort with him. And if he *was* making an effort, even a small effort, Hawk was open to it. He wanted his little girl to have a strong relationship with all of the Brands, particularly her grandparents. No, it wasn't Daintree Downs, and it never would be, but Hawk had seen Jessie's point of view. Debra Yvonne would be surrounded by family here; in the Australian outback, she would really only have her parents and ranch workers. She would need to be homeschooled and would never have the wealth of playmates, her own cousins, right here on Sugar Creek.

"Well," Jock said, rocking back on his heels, "I'm heading to a swap meet. Farm equipment."

There was a pause between them, and Jock looked at him almost expectantly. When he didn't answer the older man, Jock cleared his throat again and then said, "Are you busy right this second?"

"No," Hawk said, and he heard the caution in his voice.

"Well—" Jock scratched his ear and then his chin "—I could use a hand."

Hawk was sure that he had a confused look on his face. Was Jock actually asking him to go to the swap meet with him?

"Did you hear me, son?" Jock finally asked.

Hawk nodded.

"I'd like you to come with me to the swap meet. I've got some heavy stuff in my truck, and I'm not as young as I used to be. Can you come or not?"

Hawk nodded again.

Jock frowned at him, waved his hand for Hawk to follow, then turned on his heel and marched with slightly bowed legs back to his antique gold truck.

"Door's busted," Jock said from behind the wheel. "Just reach in and open it from the inside."

The truck, over twenty-five years old, had probably once been the pinnacle of comfort, but now it it had seen better days. Hawk was literally elbow to elbow with Jock.

Jock drove the back roads of Sugar Creek like he could do it with his eyes closed; the man was a mystery to Hawk. He obviously loved the trappings of success—his house was a log cabin mansion and his garage was filled with luxury cars—but he often preferred to drive his old beater with its dings and dents and broken doors.

"So, Jessie tells me that your grandfather's been in the hospital."

Hawk stared out to the fields on his right. He didn't really like to talk about his grandfather, not even to Jessie. He *really* didn't want to discuss him with Jock. But the last thing he needed was to take ten steps back when Jock had just taken a couple of steps forward.

"He was. But he's home now."

"Good news." Jock nodded. "Good news. Glad to hear it."

He wished he could go see his grandfather. But as they'd suspected, before he could ask for special permission to leave the country prior to receiving his green card, they would have to get married. Jessie didn't want to get married in the courthouse and Judge Silvernail, a longtime family friend who had played a pivotal role in the Brand family, had retired. While the priest had originally agreed to marry them at Callie's rehearsal, now they had to get married sooner. Jessie had remembered that Bruce had become ordained to perform marriage ceremonies to officiate for one of his best friends. When she had asked him to marry her to Hawk he hadn't hesitated to agree. Bruce had told Jessie, he was the one who put them together and it made sense for him to be the one to make it legal.

They had a person to marry them and a venue, the main house at Sugar Creek Ranch. But there was still one dark cloud hanging over the upcoming nuptials: Jessie's father had refused to give them his blessing. They'd go forward without it if they needed to, especially with his grandfather in declining health, but it was important to Jessie and to Hawk.

After Jock inquired about his grandfather, the conversation stopped, and they drove a ways down the road in their typical awkward silence. Hawk's phone rang and it was Jessie.

"Hey, honey."

"Hi," she said, her voice full of cheer. "Where are you?"

"I'm going with your father to a swap meet."

There was a shocked silence on the other end of the line. "Are you serious?"

It was such close quarters that Jock heard his daughter's words. "I'm not going to kill him and bury him in the woods, baby girl." That seemed to tickle Jock, and he chuckled to himself as he drove.

"Well, I guess that's *some* improvement in the relationship," Jessie said playfully.

"So, how's wedding planning?" Hawk changed the subject, still feeling uncomfortable being in such tight quarters with Jock.

She sighed. "Okay, I guess. Ninety days is was quick, and now that we have to move it up, it's even harder. But I think Mom and I have gotten all of the main things taken care of. I just hope you like what we've put together. I know it's rushed, but I want us to look nice."

"Okay," Hawk agreed. "Look, as long as I'm married to you at the end of the day, I'm fine with everything else, so don't worry about that."

"I love you," Jessie said.

"I love you."

Hawk was about to hang up with Jessie when the truck started to drift into the left lane.

"Bloody hell!" Hawk exclaimed. Jock had grabbed for his chest with his left arm, he had broken into a swea, and he appeared to have passed out.

Hawk dropped the phone, grabbed the steering wheel and got them back into their lane. He could hear Jessie yelling through the phone. He yelled back so she could hear him.

"Jock passed out! I've got to get us stopped."

Jock wasn't pressing on the gas, so the truck was slowing down. Hawk struggled to unbuckle his seat belt and then straddled the console so he could use his left leg and foot to reach the brake. He guided the truck onto the side of the road, braked, managed to get the truck into Park and then shut off the engine.

"Jock!" Hawk shook the older man's arm gently but firmly. "Jock!"

When he didn't respond, Hawk grabbed his phone

on the way out of the passenger side, put it on speaker and raced to the driver's side.

"What's going on?" Jessie asked fearfully. "What's wrong with Dad?"

"I think he's had a heart attack."

"A *heart attack*?"

"I think so."

"Should I call for an ambulance?" Jessie asked.

"Yes!" Hawk looked around for a mile marker and told her their location. "Then call me back."

Hawk reached into the cab and opened the door. He felt for a pulse but didn't find one.

"Damn it, Jock!" He reclined the driver's seat as far back as it would go and started CPR. "Don't you die on me!"

His phone started to ring, but he couldn't stop CPR to answer it. Hawk worked on Jock, thirty chest compressions, two rescue breaths, and then he repeated it. In the background, the phone rang again. A passerby pulled off in front of the truck, and a middle-aged man jumped out.

"Do you need some help?" The man ran over.

"Do you know CPR?" Hawk asked, his arms starting to fatigue.

"Yes."

Hawk stepped back and let the man take a turn.

"Jock Brand," the man said, shocked.

"You know him?"

"He's a lodge brother," he said, pressing on Jock's chest.

Hawk answered Jessie's third call. "They're on their way. What's going on?"

"I was giving CPR," he told her. "A lodge brother is helping me."

"CPR?" Jessie's voice was shaky and stressed.

"I've got to go, Jessie," Hawk told her.

"I'm coming."

Hawk nodded even though she couldn't see him do it. He jumped in to take a turn, all the while talking to Jock. "Jock! Come on, Jock!"

After two more turns, they got a pulse, and then finally, Jock's eyes opened a bit.

"What the hell are you doing?" Jessie's father asked in a breathy, weak, barely audible voice.

Even coming back from the dead, the man was salty.

"You're having a heart attack," Hawk said honestly.

Jock tried to sit up, but Hawk held him down firmly. "Don't move, Jock. The ambulance is on its way."

Jock didn't put up a fight; he closed his eyes, his breathing shallow.

"Thank you." Hawk held out his hand to the man who had stopped. "I really needed the help."

"I was happy to do it," the man said, shaking Hawk's hand. "I'm Beau."

"Hawk."

"Ah, yes," Beau said, "I've heard about you."

"Not one bit good I would suspect."

"No," Beau acknowledged. "But I suspect that may change."

* * *

Lilly and Jessie pulled up at the same time the ambulance arrived. The paramedics got Jock out of the truck and onto a stretcher. Once he was loaded into the ambulance, Lilly climbed in to be with her husband.

"Thank you, Uncle Beau." Jessie quickly hugged her father's friend and Masonic brother. "You've got great timing."

Beau gave Jessie a bear hug before he said, "Let me know what's going on. All of his lodge brothers will want to know."

"I will!" Jessie said, running back to the Jeep. Hawk shook Beau's hand and said one last "thank you" before he jumped into Jock's truck and followed Jessie's car.

Jessie caught up with the ambulance and followed it, at a safe distance, all the way to the hospital. After they parked, they both walked into the emergency room arm in arm. They sat down in the waiting area. Jessie sent a group family text to all her siblings about what had happened.

A flurry of messages came back in response, and Jessie knew that it was only a matter of time before all of the family members—or those that were able and in town—would show up at the hospital.

Hawk sat quietly beside her. His body was still but his mind seemed to be whirling.

"You saved him, Hawk." Jessie had taken a break from furious texting; she linked her arm with his and gazed up at him with a renewed admiration.

"I had help."

"You saved him," Jessie repeated, new tears pouring onto her cheeks.

Hawk pulled some tissues out of a box on the table next to him and dabbed her tears away.

"If you hadn't been checking on Beauty and Lucky." Jessie took the offered tissues. "If Dad hadn't asked you to go to the swap meet with him…"

"I know, love." Hawk put his arm around her shoulders and held her close. "But, I did and he did."

"Thank you," she said, holding on to him tightly, "for everything."

"I love you, Jess. Your family is my family."

"Any news?" Shane, one of her older brothers, strode into the waiting room.

Jessie stood up and hugged him tightly, happy to see him.

"They're taking him up to a room," she said. "It was a heart attack."

Shane nodded his head, unemotional. He was wearing a denim jacket with Army patches and an Army baseball cap. Shane was an incredible singer-songwriter, a veteran and a man who struggled with PTSD and his sobriety. He also was a loyal husband, a dedicated stepfather and a doting new father. Just that day, Jessie had asked Shane to sing at their wedding ceremony.

Hawk stood up and shook Shane's hand.

"Thank you, brother," Shane said to her fiancé.

"No worries, mate."

"You always seem to be coming to our rescue," her brother added.

Jessie wrapped her arms around Hawk's waist. "I told you he was a good one."

"Yes, you did." Shane sat down in a chair opposite them.

"Did you get in touch with Gabe?" she asked him, sitting back down.

Shane nodded. "And Hunter. Liam's out in Three Forks, and he's got two more stops there. I told him that we'll hold the fort while he keeps on schedule. Folks out that way wait an awfully long time to see him."

They waited several more long, grueling hours while her brothers arrived one by one. Finally, Lilly came down from Jock's room, her eyes red and puffy.

The family surrounded the matriarch, hugging her and giving her support.

"Your father's stable but will need surgery. He's going to be transferred to Providence in Missoula, and I will go with him," Lilly said.

"Missoula?" Colt asked. "What?"

"They have minimally invasive surgery for what he needs," Lilly explained. "Your father could be back home in one to two weeks."

Lilly turned her attention to Hawk. "We could have lost him today if Hawk hadn't been with him. What started as a heart attack led to cardiac arrest." Lilly took both of his hands in hers and looked up into his face. "You are a blessing to this family,

Hawk. This isn't the first time you've come to my rescue."

Then Lilly hugged him tightly and Jessie felt grateful and so relieved that her family was embracing Hawk. Now, if only Hawk's grandfather could embrace their choices, everything in their lives would fall into place.

"When can we see him?" Colt asked.

"Now," Lilly said. "One at a time though. I want him to stay calm."

Then, much to everyone's surprise, Lilly said, "Jock wants to see you first, Hawk."

"I don't think I should be first." Hawk shook his head.

"It's what he wants," Lilly said in a tone that brooked no argument.

"Yes, ma'am," Hawk said. And then when Lilly gave him a sour look, he fixed his words. "Yes, Lilly."

Lilly linked her arm with his as Jessie always did. He gave his fiancée a quick kiss on the lips, then followed Lilly to the elevators. They rode up quietly; when they reached the floor, Hawk's chest began to pound nervously. Even now, he couldn't stop feeling nervous about seeing Jock. The one person he wanted to approve of him, Jessie's father, had never given him his blessing to marry his daughter. But actually, he understood the elder man's point; he might be younger than Jock by several decades, but he was old-fashioned enough to believe in marriage first, baby second.

"I'll leave you two alone," Lilly said.

Jock was hooked up to a lot of machines and had an oxygen mask on. Jock moved his fingers to signal that Hawk should come closer. Hawk walked over and took a seat in the chair that had been positioned near the bed.

Jock pulled his mask down; Hawk tried to stop him. But Jock was still his stubborn self and did as he pleased.

"Thank you," Jock said to him, his voice very weak and raspy. "You saved my life."

"You're welcome, Jock." Hawk gave a nod of his head. "You are important to Jessie, so you're important to me."

Jock pulled up the mask for a minute or two before he pulled it back down. "I was afraid that you were going to take my little girl back to Australia."

Hawk didn't respond; he just listened.

"But I see how much you love my baby girl."

"With all of my heart."

Jock took a break to get some oxygen; then he continued.

"And I see how much she loves you."

"I'm a lucky man."

Jock's eyes fluttered shut for a second, and Hawk leaned forward, worried. Jock coughed several times behind the mask, his eyes still closed.

"I should let you get some rest," Hawk said.

Jock shook his head and then opened his eyes.

"We can talk later," he said to Jock.

"No," Jock said, pulling down the mask again. "Now. What I've got to say can't wait. I need to say this now."

Chapter Thirteen

Jock may be *temporarily* down for the count, but he was the leader of the Brand family and Hawk's senior—he deserved his respect. If Jock wanted to talk now, Hawk was willing to listen.

Jock looked at him with deep-set blue eyes—Jessie's eyes—and wordlessly, the older man held out his hand.

Hawk looked at the outstretched hand; this was the moment he had been waiting for, and it was hard to believe that the moment was actually here.

"Welcome to the family, Hawk," Jock said, his voice raspy.

"Thank you, sir."

The handshake over, Jock didn't let go of his hand. The elder leaned forward a bit and said, "You have my blessing to marry my daughter."

Stunned, it took him a minute to respond, but all he could think to say was a repeat of his early words. "Thank you, sir."

Jock nodded as he slipped the oxygen back on. He closed his eyes and breathed in deeply. Then he took the mask off again.

"She's my only daughter."

"Yes, sir."

"Promise me…" Jock started to cough again, so loudly that Lilly came into the room.

"Save your breath, love." Lilly went to the other side of the bed and put her hands on her husband's arm and shoulder.

"No," Jock said stubbornly, "I need to say this now. Tomorrow waits for no man."

Hawk stood up, aware that there was a waiting room full of Brands wanting to see their father.

"Hawk?"

"Yes, sir."

"Promise me that, no matter what, you'll take care of our Jessie for the rest of her life."

"I will, sir."

"I don't want Jessie to leave Montana."

"That's not the plan."

"I want her to stay at Sugar Creek. Breed those quarter horses. Build on her stake."

"I want that for her too."

"But if *you do*…" Jock tried to sit up a bit.

"Jock." Lilly held on to her husband's arm. "Calm yourself, please."

"Take her away, I expect—" Jock paused to catch his breath "—an open invitation at that cattle station of yours."

"It's not the plan. But of course. All of the Brands will always be welcome at Daintree Downs."

Once Jock had finally said his piece, Hawk went down to the waiting room. Shane was the next to go up to see his father.

"What happened?" Jessie asked, anxiously. "How's Dad?"

"Still in charge," Hawk reported. "You wouldn't think he'd just had a near-death experience."

"That's good to hear." Jessie hugged him. "What did he want to say to you?"

"Thank you. And welcome to the family."

"Are you *serious*?" Jessie's pretty eyes widened with surprise.

"Yes." He kissed his beautiful fiancée on the lips. "Today, I earned your father's respect, and he gave me the one thing I've needed the most—he gave me his blessing to marry you."

Jock returned to his beloved Sugar Creek Ranch two weeks after his surgery. He still needed to regain his strength, but he was as surly as he had been before the heart attack; that surliness was a sign to the family that Jock was on the road to being back to himself. The wedding planning had continued in his absence. Jessie, Lilly, Kate and Callie had worked furiously to put the final touches on the great room in the main house, which featured incredibly high ceilings with large wood beams sourced from Sugar Creek, a wall of floor-to-ceiling windows, acres of bucolic pastureland and dramatic mountain peaks far off in the distance. When Jessie was a little girl, she had imagined marrying her Montana man in the great room. As it turned out, she wasn't going to marry a Montana cowboy; instead, her husband-to-be was a sexy outback rancher.

"How are you feeling?" Bruce asked her.

Now that the bulk of the pop-up wedding planning was done, Jessie decided to get out into the fresh Montana air.

"I'm good." She smiled at him.

"How about you?" she asked her oldest brother. "Are you ready to marry me off to Hawk?"

Bruce laughed. "I think you'll be in good hands."

"He is a good one, isn't he?"

Her brother glanced over at Hawk. "I'd say so. I mean, for him to give up his birthright, his claim on Daintree Downs—I don't doubt for a second that he's here for the right reasons."

Jessie's chest tightened. "What do you mean *give up* his claim to Daintree Downs?"

What did Bruce know that she *didn't*?

Her brother looked at her, and she could plainly read on his face that he had said something that he wished that he could rewind and erase.

"I've said too much, I think."

"No," she said, "you haven't said enough."

"I'm not going to betray Hawk's confidence," Bruce said, "more than I already have."

Suddenly, Jessie felt queasy. She had believed that she was his best friend and first confidant. It was a horrible feeling to discover that she was wrong about that—particularly so close to the wedding date. Finding out that Hawk had been keeping a major secret from her while confiding in her brother made her question, for the first time, her decision to marry him so quickly. There was a large dent in her unwavering trust in Hawk that hadn't been there before. In three days, they would be married. Did she really *know* Hawk well enough to marry him? She loved him, of course, but was that really enough?

"There you are." Hawk walked through the front door onto the porch.

Ever since she had found out about Hawk's secret, Jessie hadn't been able to think of much else, and the more she thought about it, the angrier she became. She had become quiet and introspective, and she knew that Hawk had noticed.

"Can I join you?" he asked.

Jessie nodded and made room on the porch swing for him. After he sat down, neither of them spoke. Hawk was the one to break the silence between them.

"Jessie," he said in a measured tone, "what is going on here? Are you having second thoughts?"

She didn't look at him while she mulled over what she should say in response.

"Yes," Jessie said honestly, "I am."

Jessie could see the stunned expression on Hawk's face from the corner of her eye. Her fiancé turned his body toward her, his eyes locked on her face.

"You have to talk to me, Jessie," he said. "What's wrong? What's changed?"

Still not willing to look at him, she said, "You've been lying to me."

"Lying to you?" His tone elevated.

"Yes," she repeated. "Lying to me."

"About what?"

That was when she looked him right in the eyes. "Bruce let your secret slip out."

At first, there was confusion in Hawk's moss green eyes, but then realization dawned.

"I see," he said.

"That's it? You see?" she snapped. "I've been asking you for weeks what's wrong, and you kept on telling me that I knew everything I needed to know!"

"That wasn't a lie."

"It wasn't?" Jessie asked furiously. "Your grandfather is disinheriting you, and you didn't think I needed to know that?"

"That's right."

"In what actual universe does that make sense, Hawk? I would never ask you to give up Daintree Downs. I always thought that we would live in both worlds! We would have a home here on Sugar Creek and a home on Daintree Downs."

Hawk just listened while she continued.

"Is this a done deal?" she asked. "Have you lost Daintree Downs forever because of me?"

"Not because of you."

"*Yes*, because of me."

Hawk took a deep breath in through his nose and let it out slowly. "This is exactly why I didn't tell you. I didn't want you to get upset. It's not healthy for you or our baby. Especially when there was nothing you could do about it."

"I'm not a child."

"I never said that you were."

"I'm not a fragile little flower who can't handle things either!"

"That never crossed my mind," he said, frustration creeping into his voice. "But you are carrying our child. *Your health*, our *baby's* health, is more important to me than anything, and that includes Daintree Downs."

Tears that she had been holding back ever since she had found out about Hawk's secret flowed freely onto her cheeks now. It had never occurred to her that his grandfather would take such drastic measures. Yes, she knew that he was angry and disappointed, but to take the cattle station from Hawk, that had been unthinkable to her. It was the true worst-case scenario.

Hawk put his arm around her shoulders and drew her close. "Please don't cry, my love."

"What will happen to Daintree Downs?" she asked, wiping the tears from her face and forcing herself to stop crying. Hawk didn't need her tears right now; he needed her support.

"It will be donated to the state of Queensland."

When she had first met Hawk, when he had taken her on a helicopter tour of the vast cattle station holdings, he had explained to her that Australia's large cattle stations were being bought en masse by foreign governments and that keeping Daintree Downs in the hands of Australians was more important to him that anything. The fact that Hawk was the descendent of Australia's First Peoples *and* stood to inherit a massive cattle station was a source of pride for him.

"You should have told me." Jessie turned her body toward him and took his hands in hers.

"I was trying to protect you," he said sincerely. "But I see now that I should have told you. I'm sorry you found out the way you did. I'm sorry that I didn't tell you straightaway."

"Thank you," she said. "I forgive you. But, please, in the future, I need to be the first to know."

"Agreed," he said, a relieved look in his eyes.

They kissed and made up, and then Jessie asked, "Is there any way to fix this, Hawk? Any way to change your grandfather's mind?"

"I don't know," he said honestly. "Athena told me he changed his will, but he has refused to answer my calls. Or maybe Athena has possession of his phone. I just don't know. Until I can get back to Australia, I can't really gauge the situation."

"You don't…" Jessie started a thought but paused

before she continued. "You don't think that your grandfather would leave it to Athena do you?"

"No," Hawk said quietly. "That crossed my mind, but no. I don't."

"Well, as soon as we are married in two days, we will petition immigration to let you return to Australia."

"Yes," he agreed.

"And if we have to move to Australia to keep you from losing your birthright, then that's what we will have to do," Jessie said, sounding more confident for Hawk's sake than she actually felt on the inside. The thought of living such an isolated life in the Australian outback didn't appeal to her. It never had.

"I don't think that's the best idea for you or our child, Jessie," Hawk said. "I didn't know what was so special about Montana, but now I do. Here, we will be surrounded by family. In Australia, we will really only have ourselves."

"I want you to be happy, Hawk," she said. "If you lose the cattle station, you won't be happy. Not really. And I would never be happy knowing that our relationship was the reason you lost something so important to you."

Hawk pulled her closer still; his arm around her seemed to be as much for his comfort as hers. "You don't understand, my love, I don't get my happiness from the cattle station anymore. I get my happiness from you."

Theirs was a late afternoon wedding. The great room was filled with light, and the space was perfect for an intimate event. Callie made a perfect maid of honor and Liam served as Hawk's best man. Most of her family was able to attend in person, with Hunter and Skyler virtual through video chat. Jessie had also invited several childhood friends who completed the guest list.

Her greatest joy was the fact that her father, still regaining his strength, was there to walk her down the aisle. Hawk watched them both keenly, his eyes full of acceptance and love.

Jock had tears in his eyes, something Jessie had never seen before, when her father kissed her on the cheek and then symbolically put her hand into Hawk's hand.

"Take care of her," Jock said and held out his hand.

Hawk shook his hand. "I will, sir. For the rest of my life."

Once she was standing in her spot, facing her soon-to-be husband, Hawk said, "You look absolutely stunning, my love."

"Thank you," she said. "You look so handsome."

"Are you guys finished admiring each other?" Bruce asked teasingly. "Or are you ready to get hitched?"

"We're ready to get hitched," they said in unison and then laughed, as did their guests.

The ceremony was short and sweet and to the

point; they got to the "You may kiss the bride" part in record time.

Hawk kissed her several times before he offered her his arm. "Mrs. Bowhill."

She linked her arm with his happily. "My husband."

Together, they walked past their guests, and Jessie felt like she would never forget this exact moment, when her family and friends were cheering for them and throwing confetti. At the end of the short aisle, Hawk took her into his arms, dipped her dramatically and then brought her up for one final kiss. The photographer, who they found on short notice, captured the moment.

"We did it," Hawk said after he kissed her.

"Yes, we did." Jessie was smiling so hard that her cheeks had begun to hurt. She couldn't remember ever feeling this happy.

It seemed that even Mother Nature was supportive of their union; the plan to have an outdoor reception, weather permitting, went off without a hitch. The weather was perfect for an outdoor meal, and as the sun began to set on the horizon, Jessie and her husband moved from table to table, sharing moments with their family and her friends. After everyone felt stuffed from the wedding feast, coffee and bourbon was served and, under the twinkling lights that had been strung up for ambience, Hawk and Jessie shared their first dance as a married couple.

"I feel happy." Hawk leaned down to touch his forehead to hers.

"So do I."

"Until I met you, I didn't know what true love was."

Jessie kissed her husband, and then she laughed when he twirled her around, making the skirt of her dress billow out in the most pleasing way. Hawk brought her back toward his body, his strong arm holding her as he dipped her.

At the end of the song, Jessie saw her father walking toward them. Jock tapped Hawk on the shoulder.

"I'd like to have a dance with my daughter," her father said, bringing a swell of emotion rushing into her heart.

"Yes, sir." Hawk stepped back to make room for the elder.

"I'm proud to know you, son," her father said.

For Jessie, that was the biggest stamp of approval her father could have given to her new husband.

"Are you happy?" her father asked, rather awkwardly moving them in a small circle.

"Beyond."

"Do you love him?"

"More than words."

"Does he love you?"

"More than words."

Her father's deep-set blue eyes were wet with emotion. "Do you know how much I love you?"

Jessie flung her arms around her father's neck,

tears of joy in her eyes, halting their dance. "More than words."

At the end of the night, after most of the guests had gone home, the family members, a bit tipsy from expensive champagne and strong bourbon, headed to the guest rooms, of which there were plenty. Jessie and Hawk drove the short distance to Hunter and Skyler's hobby farm and walked hand in hand to the front porch. Hawk, ever the romantic and old-fashioned guy, carried her over the threshold into the house. He put her down gently, sweetly, and they shared a kiss in the small foyer. They slowly made their way to the bedroom, both feeling overwhelmed by the success of their impromptu wedding. Everyone was happy for them; everyone was in good cheer and wished them well for their future together. Even Hunter and Skyler were incredibly supportive and excited, especially in the face of their own horrible news.

With her hand on her belly, Jessie asked, "Can we still consummate our marriage when we have so obviously already *consummated* hundreds of times *before* the nuptials?"

He smiled that devilishly handsome smile of his; a real knockout smile that made her knees feel a bit weak every single time he flashed it at her. "We were just practicing for the main event."

"Well," she said in her sexiest voice, "then I have something special for tonight."

She turned around so he could unzip her gown

for her; he dropped loving kisses on the bare skin of her back, sending a lovely tingling sensation up her spine.

When he was finished with his task, she sashayed to the bathroom door, looking over her shoulder at him playfully. "But no peeking."

Hawk covered his eyes with his hand and then moved his fingers aside so he could peek through space.

She laughed at him before she went into the bathroom. "No peeking!"

Excitedly, Jessie stripped out of her wedding gown, hung it up on a hanger that she had left hanging on the shower curtain rod and then searched behind a stack of towels for the bag she had hidden there days before.

She opened the bag and fished out the slinky lingerie she had purchased from the wedding shop where she had purchased her gown. Hawk was a man who appreciated the tease. He didn't want to see everything blatantly on display. He preferred the mystery and the fun of unwrapping the gift she had for him inside. Knowing that, she had purchased a silky long nighty with a lace bodice with a deep V and a high slit for her leg to peek out in an enticing way. The slinky material of the nighty skated over her growing baby bump, not hiding it but enhancing it.

Jessie washed the makeup off her face and took the bobby pins out of her hair so it fell naturally down her back. Hawk loved to comb his fingers through her hair; she wanted to do everything she could to make this night, their wedding night, their first time as husband and wife, to be the most memorable night of their lives.

At the bathroom door, she called out to him, "Are you ready, Mr. Bowhill?"

When he didn't respond, a worried crease marred her forehead as she opened the door. "I swear, Hawk Bowhill, if you've fallen asleep on me, I will never forgive you…"

She opened the door and walked into the bedroom. Hawk wasn't asleep, but he was sitting on the edge of the bed, seemingly frozen, staring at his phone.

"Hawk?" She walked over to him quickly. "Are you okay?"

He still didn't respond to her, his eyes glued to the screen of his phone.

She sat down next to him on the bed and put her arm around his shoulders. "What's wrong? What's happened? Talk to me."

In a rough whisper that sounded almost strangled by the emotion in his voice, Hawk said, "My grandfather has died."

Chapter Fourteen

It took several moments for the news to register in Jessie's brain; it took several minutes for her to formulate any rational response.

"How?" One word was all she could manage to get out. "When?"

Of all the days, of all of the moments, this was news that would forever be a scar on an otherwise perfect day. It was unfathomable; it was so unfair.

"In his sleep," Hawk said. "Yesterday."

"How kind of Athena to wait until our wedding day to tell you."

"She said that he died of a broken heart."

Jessie was furious, and she couldn't stop that anger from showing up in her tone when she said, "*Horrid* woman!"

The only thing Jessie could think to do was to wrap her arms around Hawk and hold him tightly. Her mind was jumbled with racing thoughts, decrying the injustice of Hawk not being able to say goodbye to his grandfather and wishing that she could rewind the clock and do so many things differently. If she hadn't insisted on making their lives in Montana, Hawk wouldn't have been estranged from his grandfather. None of this would have happened.

"I'm so sorry, Hawk," she said. "This is my fault."

"No, it's not." His response was quick and swift. "I will not let you take that on."

The last thing Jessie wanted to do was upset her husband more, so she dropped the self-blame and focused on Hawk.

"What should we do now?" she asked him, her arm linked with his, her hand resting on top of his.

"I need to go to Australia."

She nodded. "We'll get in touch with our immigration lawyer first thing."

Hawk turned toward her and lifted up her chin so she was looking directly into her eyes. "This isn't your fault, Jessie. I don't want you upset. You're carrying our child, our future, and I can't have you depressed or sad or filled with remorse. It's not good for you or our little girl. Promise me."

Jessie didn't think she could make that promise; in her mind, there was a very straight line connecting Hawk's fracture in the relationship with his grandfather to her insistence of making their home at Sugar Creek.

When she broke eye contact, Hawk wouldn't have it.

"Look at me, Jessie," he said, his tone strong and insistent.

She brought her gaze back to his, and he said, "Promise me."

"Okay," she finally said, "I will try my best."

Seeming more like himself and more in charge of his emotions, Hawk sealed their deal with a kiss and then drew her close to his body.

"You are the most important thing to me. You and our child," he said, still holding her close. "You are the only family I have left."

"I love you, Hawk," she said, not able to hold back her tears. "More than anything or anyone in this world."

And it was that moment that Jessie knew what she had to do. It was then that she realized how much Hawk loved her and how much he had been willing to sacrifice to ensure her happiness. Now, it was her turn to do the same for him. She was a wife and would be a mother soon; it was time for her to grow up.

Hawk woke up the day after his wedding later than he had slept in years. The bed was empty beside him, and that made him concerned. He quickly got dressed, went downstairs and called out for his wife, only to realize that she wasn't in the house at all. At the front door, he tugged on his boots, put on the Stetson his wife had purchased for him when he arrived in Montana—an event that seemed like a lifetime ago—and went outside. It was looking like it was going to turn out to be a sunny day, but the weather wasn't foremost on his mind. He was concerned mainly about Jessie. The shock of his grandfather's passing had hit her hard. He had held her late into the night while she cried periodically. He knew, because he knew Jessie better than he knew himself, that she was crying for him—for his lost relationship with his grandfather, for their daughter who would never meet her great-grandfather. Jessie had always been a sensitive woman; it didn't surprise him, really, that she had taken this hard.

Hawk headed for the first place he thought his wife would be: the barn. Dream Chaser, a pretty little mare that Jessie had barrel-raced with as a teenager, was now Skyler's beloved trail horse. Ever since they had moved to Hunter and Skyler's farm, Jessie had rekindled her bond with Dream Chaser. Just as he had often found solace with his animals out in the bush, Jessie had found comfort in spending time with Dream.

"Good morning, my love," he said once he found Jessie.

She gave him a brief smile before she accepted a good-morning kiss from him. Her eyes were puffy from a night of crying; her skin, which was usually glowing and vibrant, had an ashy undertone.

"Good morning." Jessie continued to brush Dream's coat. She had the mare in the crossties, grooming her as she had gotten in the habit of doing.

"Did you see the text from our attorney?" she asked.

He leaned back against the wooden wall, wishing that his pretty wife wasn't so somber.

"Yes. Meeting at 10:00 a.m."

"It was her first available. I have a feeling she moved some things around to accommodate us."

"Okay."

"Did you get breakfast?"

"No," he said, "the first thing I did was come to find you."

"Here I am," she said with another weak, half-hearted smile.

Hawk felt uneasy in his gut; he just didn't know how to console her. What could he say to make her snap out of the negative space she had gone to in her head? After a couple of long minutes of silence between them, Hawk said, "You've got to talk to me, sweetheart. Chances are, I'm going back to Australia to bury my grandfather. But I can't leave if you are like this…"

"Like what?" she asked defensively.

"Jessie. Come on," he said, fatigue and frustration laced in his tone.

Wordlessly, Jessie unhooked Dream from the

crossties and took the mare back to the stall. After she hung up the horse's halter in the hook just outside the stall, Jessie stepped into his open embrace and hugged him tightly.

"How are you today?" she asked, her head tucked beneath his chin.

"Worried about you."

"I'm worried about you," she said.

He held her away from him so he could look into her face. "I'll be fine if *you* are okay."

"I'm trying, Hawk," Jessie said. "I really am. I was up all night. I just couldn't seem to shut my brain off."

"Let's go back to the house."

Together, each with an arm around the other's back, they walked out of the barn toward the house. Jessie put a pot of coffee on; once it was ready, she poured a cup for him, and they went out to the porch to sit on the swing.

"I'm sorry, Hawk."

"Jessie…" He said her name with a good dose of frustration.

"No, Hawk." She put her hand on his leg. "Hear me out."

He looked at his beloved's face, and he could read on her pinched, stressed features that she had something to get off her chest; he needed to listen to her. When she realized that he was waiting for her to speak and that she had his undivided attention, Jessie continued.

"I've been thinking all night. All night. And the

one thing that I keep on returning to again and again is that I have been in denial. I was in denial because I wanted to fit you into this box that I had built in my mind about how my life would be when I grew up. I always saw my life as a wife and a mother on my stake on Sugar Creek. It's all I've ever wanted. So, when I met you, I didn't want to think about all that you had in Australia. I turned a blind eye to it, really, because I wanted the dream—all of those childhood dreams—to come true."

She looked up at him with deep, dark sapphire blue eyes so full of remorse that it broke his heart. "But you don't fit into that box, Hawk."

He took her hand and kissed it. "Yes, I do."

She shook her head slowly. "No, you don't."

The last twenty-four hours had been a roller coaster—the high of marrying the woman he loved more than life itself and losing the man who raised him after his parents died in a tragic car accident. Now, his gut was twisting into a knot because something had changed in Jessie's inner world; he was almost afraid of what she was going to say next. If she couldn't imagine him with her on Sugar Creek, what did that mean for their future as a married couple—as parents to Debra Yvonne?

"You belong to Daintree Downs." Those were her next words.

"I belong with you." He held on to her hand just a bit tighter. "We belong together."

"Daintree Downs holds your spirit, Hawk. Sugar Creek can never be that for you."

He couldn't deny the truth of her words, so he didn't try to.

She put her free hand on top of their joined hands and looked up into his face so sincerely. "I'm sorry I didn't come to this realization sooner. If I had, your grandfather might very well be alive."

"No," Hawk said firmly. "That's not your burden to shoulder. I made the choice, not you."

"I didn't give you much of a choice, Hawk. Leave your country or leave your child?" she said, still holding on to his hand. "I can't go back..."

"No."

"But I can find a better path forward," his wife said. "After Callie's wedding, I am going to pack what needs to be packed so I can move to Australia with you."

It was odd, but when his wife said the very words he had wanted to hear for months and months, his brain seemed unable to process the message. The words were floating around in his head like dust balls being pushed around by a soft breeze. Perhaps it was difficult to process because, after having spent time with the Brand family and growing to love Sugar Creek, Hawk just wasn't so certain that Daintree Downs *was* the best place for his daughter to grow up. In truth, Jessie and he had changed sides. She was on Team Australia and he was on Team Montana.

"I don't know about that, Jessie."

"I do." She jutted her chin out stubbornly. "I can't—no, I *won't* be the reason you lose your birthright."

Realizing that his wife was dug into her overnight decision, Hawk decided to give in, for now, but in his mind, the possibility of moving to Australia permanently was a huge question mark for him.

"First, I need to get permission to go back to Australia."

"If they don't give you permission," Jessie said, her voice elevated, "then, you'll go anyway, green card be damned."

It wasn't so cut and dried, and they both knew it. While Jessie could fly internationally up to twenty-eight weeks, neither of them felt like it was a good idea for her to travel with him back to Australia right now. The isolation of Daintree Downs would take her too far away from medical care. Plus, if he left the country without permission, he could get stuck in Australia and miss the birth of his first child. No matter what the cost, he couldn't live with that outcome.

Not wanting to argue the point with Jessie, Hawk put his arm around her and drew her into his embrace. That seemed to soothe her, and in turn, it managed to soothe him as well.

"Do you forgive me?" she whispered.

"There's nothing to forgive."

"Do you forgive me?"

"Will it make you feel better if I do?" he asked,

just wanting to find a way to make her feel better. When she hurt, he hurt.

"Yes."

"Then I forgive you."

She tightened her arms around him. "Thank you."

"I love you, Jess." He said the words he knew he would be saying every day for the rest of his life.

"I love you, Hawk."

He kissed her on the top of her head. "That's all I need, my love. With your love, I can achieve amazing things."

Five days into their marriage, Jessie was driving Hawk to the airport so he could begin his journey back to Brisbane. At first, it was a relief that they had been granted special permission for him to travel back to Australia, but then, reality began to sink in that he was leaving. For Jessie, that realization plus the sadness surrounding Hawk's grandfather's death was the reason they were both quiet and introspective during the ride to Bozeman International Airport. When he first heard the news, Hawk had seemed to take his grandfather's passing *too* well, but yesterday, his real emotions began to rise to the surface. Jessie had never seen Hawk truly depressed; it was difficult to know how to help him.

"I can't believe I missed the funeral," Hawk said, looking straight ahead.

"I know." She took her hand off the wheel for a

second to touch his arm. "I can't even imagine how you feel."

Daintree Downs had been in the Bowhill family for generations, and because of this historical history, the powers that be in Queensland allowed the family to maintain a burial site on cattle station property. His grandfather was laid to rest next to his grandmother the day after his death. Because there was no way to refrigerate the body, his grandfather had to be buried quickly. Athena had made all of the arrangements for the funeral, but she hadn't even sent Hawk a link so he could at least attend remotely.

"I hope you find a way to say goodbye in your own way once you're there."

Hawk nodded his head; he looked tired, with dark circles beneath his eyes. But no matter how sad he was, Jessie had every confidence that he would be able to handle any conflict that came his way. Her husband was a very resilient man; that's how outback ranchers were built.

"What's the first step?" she asked him.

"Meet with the attorney handling his estate in Brisbane. Thankfully, Grandpa didn't leave Athena in charge of his estate. If he had, there would be no point in me going back."

Based on Hawk's descriptions of his grandfather, and her limited knowledge from the time she had spent at Daintree Downs, William Bowhill had been many things in life—demanding, unbending, determined to have his own way in every situation—but the man was strategic. He wanted Hawk back in Australia and chained to the cattle station; he must have known that making Athena executor of his estate would have been a bridge too far for his grandson, who had only tolerated his relationship with Athena.

"When will you go back to Daintree Downs?" she asked, pulling into the airport parking lot.

"I've asked that my plane be serviced and fueled." Hawk opened the passenger door after she parked. "Once I'm done with the attorney and I know exactly what we're up against, I'll fly out."

At the curbside, they checked in Hawk's baggage, checked in for his flight and got his boarding pass; he was traveling light with the full intention of returning well before the baby's due date. Hand in hand, they walked slowly, stalling for time, toward the security check.

"Take care of yourself." Hawk took her face in his hands to kiss her sweetly, and then he knelt down to kiss her baby belly. "And take care of our little girl."

Jessie straightened the collar of his shirt and brushed a piece of lint off his sleeve. "You take care of yourself. Don't fly that plane if weather conditions aren't perfect. Nothing on that cattle station is worth your life."

He kissed her again. "I promise."

When there wasn't a moment left, Hawk got in line for the security check, standing sideways so he could get several final looks at her. On the other side of the metal detector, Hawk pulled on his boots, put on his Stetson and gave her one last wave and sent her a kiss through the air. Long after he had disappeared from view, Jessie was glued to her spot. It wasn't until the baby started to turn, using her ribs as a launching platform, that she came back to the present.

Her hands on her stomach, Jessie headed toward the exit. "Well, kid, it's just you and me for now."

On the way back to Sugar Creek, Jessie struggled to find the right music for the car ride. Everything seemed too cheerful and upbeat when she felt so sad. Finally, she switched off the radio and rode in silence. She was lucky that she could stay at the main house in her own suite of rooms while Hawk was gone. And she was fortunate that she had Callie's wedding planning to keep her busy and occupied. But the bottom line was that nothing was going to fill the gaping hole Hawk had left in her life and her heart. The only thing that would fill it was for them to be together again. Jessie did not care if they built their lives in Montana or Queensland—the only thing that mattered now was that they were together.

"You, me and Daddy." Jessie rested her hand on her stomach briefly. "You, me and Daddy."

"G'day, my love." Hawk called Jessie on video chat before he took off to fly back to Daintree Downs. He tried to sound and look more cheerful than he actually felt for Jessie's sake.

"Hawk!" It made him smile how happy she always was to see him, to hear his voice. "I miss you!"

"I miss you, my beautiful bride."

She smiled prettily at his compliment as she asked, "How did it go?"

Hawk gave a little shake of his head. "Let's discuss it later."

This wasn't the moment to unpack everything he had learned at the attorney's office. He was, in fact, stunned by the changes in his grandfather's will that he felt as if he needed some time to process the information.

"Oh." Jessie frowned. "Okay. That bad, huh?"

"Let's put it this way—we have a lot of decisions to make."

"Okay," she said again. "Are you heading to Daintree now?"

"Yes."

"Is the weather clear?"

He turned the phone so she could see the weather outside. "Blue skies all the way."

"Don't get distracted."

He knew she was worried that he would get distracted by the contents of his grandfather's will and forget to pay attention to his flying.

"I'll be fine," he said. "I'll call you the minute I land."

They said their goodbyes, and he loaded the bags into the plane. Once he taxied out to the runway, once he felt the exhilaration of heading down it, once he took flight, that's when he truly felt that he was back home. Brisbane had never felt like home, but the flight back to Daintree was dotted with landmarks that reminded him he was getting closer and then closer still to the land that had always filled his heart. His pulse began to beat rapidly at the first sight of the familiar terrain that let him know he was home. Every tree, every cow, every water hole was a sight for sore eyes. He hadn't even realized until this reunion how much he had missed the outback. Perhaps he had suppressed it, pushed it aside, in order to give Montana a genuine shot.

As he approached the cattle station's wide dirt runway, his body began to tingle with excitement and anticipation. It was a devastating event, the death of his grandfather, that had brought him back to his homeland. But at this exact moment, as the wheels of his plane first touched the bumpy, rugged runway and he could finally stop his forward motion, it didn't matter what had brought him back—he was home.

Hawk turned off the engine, jumped out of the plane, knelt down on one knee, dug his fingers into the dirt and brought it to his nose so he could inhale the scent of the earth beneath his feet. He sat back on his heel, his eyes trying to drink everything in.

Hawk stood up; he let the dirt from his hands fall back onto the ground as he brushed his hands across the legs of his jeans. He closed his eyes; he allowed himself a moment to just listen to the natural sounds of Daintree and catch the familiar scents.

After several minutes, Hawk grabbed his bags out of the plane and headed for a ranch truck that had been left for him at the runway by one of his most trusted employees. He didn't want Athena to know exactly when he would arrive; he wanted the element of surprise on his side. Before he headed to his next stop, Hawk called Jess. Video chat wasn't possible, but a phone call was.

"I'm glad you arrived safely," Jessie said. "How does it feel to be back?"

"It feels amazing," he said honestly but then regretted sounding so thrilled to be back on Daintree soil. "Not that I don't love Sugar Creek…"

"Hawk, you don't have to explain. Your love for that land is part of you, and I love all of you."

Chapter Fifteen

Hawk's next stop was the family burial site. The warm feeling he had in his heart seemed to turn to ice-cold water when he drove up to the small grave-yard surrounded by a wooden fence that had been built by his ancestors. He got out of the truck, but it took him a while to force himself to walk to the newly dug plot where his grandfather had been laid to rest.

Hawk took off his hat as he stood in front of his grandfather's grave. He had been buried beside his wife, Debra, but his part of the double headstone still needed to be engraved. Solemnly, Hawk knelt down in front of the grave, hat in hand, and bowed his head. Silently, he prayed that his grandfather had been reunited with his beloved wife; theirs had not been a perfect marriage, but it had been built on an abiding friendship.

"I love you both," Hawk said quietly to his grandparents. If it weren't for them taking on his upbringing when his parents died, there was no telling where he would be now. He wouldn't be married to Jessie; he wouldn't be getting ready to welcome his daughter into the world. But on the other side of that coin, he wouldn't be facing the most critical decision of his life. It seemed that no matter what Jessie and he decided, someone was going to lose.

Somehow, from their graves, his grandparents gave him a renewed strength to go on to the next stop on his route—the main house. Athena would be there; her grandfather had given her one of the guest rooms in the main house, a classic single-story structure raised with a tin roof and large verandas on all sides. Hawk knew that it would take several sticks of dynamite to get Athena to move. But one way or another, move she would.

There was an uncomfortable knot twisted up in his gut when he pulled up to his childhood home. It was the first time he'd ever felt uncomfortable going into the main house. What would it feel like now that his grandfather's giant, all-encompassing energy was gone? Slowly, Hawk walked up one of the double staircases to the veranda on the front side of the house. The familiar creaks and groans of the steps transported him back to his childhood, when he would race up those stairs to find out what his grandmother was cooking for dinner.

Hawk opened the front door of the main house; he wasn't wrong to think that it would seem muted and quiet without his grandfather's life force flowing to every corner of the home.

He was still standing near the front door, his bags in his hands, when Athena came around a corner on her way to the kitchen. "G'day, Athena."

Stunned by his voice, Athena stopped, grabbed for her chest and squeezed her eyes shut.

"Hawk!" She opened her eyes and glared at him. "You scared me half to death."

Athena looked as if she had aged ten years; her eyes were puffy from crying, and her face looked pale and gaunt.

"What are you doing here?" she snapped.

"This is my home, Athena," Hawk said in an even, commanding voice. "Meet me in my grandfather's office in ten minutes."

"I don't work for you, Hawk."

"Actually, according to my grandfather's will, you do," he told her as he brushed past her to go to the office. "Ten minutes."

Sitting in his grandfather's well-worn leather chair was something that he had done as a child, but as an adult, he never would have disrespected him in that way. It felt odd and uncomfortable to be sitting in that chair now, yet it was something that Hawk knew he had to do when he dealt with Athena.

"Have a seat." He gestured to a chair she sat in often when she was acting as his grandfather's assistant.

Athena had a sour expression on her face as she sat down in the familiar chair. She had always been a slender woman, pretty in her youth. But the years had gotten the best of Athena; she was painfully thin and her cheeks hollow. Her once thick black hair was thinning at the hairline, and she hadn't colored it in years, letting the yellowish-gray hair dominate.

"I suppose you're keen to fire me."

"Straightaway."

"Your grandfather loved me," Athena told him.

"I'm not here to debate that," Hawk said, surprised at the calmness in his own voice. "He provided for you in his will. It's more than enough for you to get a fresh start."

"Of course you want me to leave," Athena seethed. "You never liked me."

He didn't respond; it was the truth. No sense rehashing it.

Athena stood up, her sunken eyes blazing. "He wouldn't marry me because of you."

The longer he was silent, the madder it seemed to make her. "You *gutted* him when you left. You were the death of him, Pengana. The *death* of him!"

On her way out of the office, Athena stopped, her

hands balled up by her side: "I was his mistress long before Debra died. It had been going on for *years*!"

Hawk stood up, his back ramrod straight. Athena had been holding on to that grenade, just waiting for the right moment to lob it at him. She wanted to cause the most damage and pain she could; she had always blamed him for her grandfather's unwillingness to marry her.

Hands on the top of his grandfather's desk, Hawk said without a drop of emotion in his voice, "That's old news, Athena." And it was.

Athena seemed stunned that her hand grenade had turned out to be a dud. Hawk almost felt sorry for her when he saw tears of frustration and anger in her eyes. But then he thought of his grandmother, a woman who had loved his grandfather so dearly and completely, blissfully unaware of her husband's infidelities.

Hawk had found out about the affair quite by accident when he was sixteen; he had seen Athena and his grandfather walk hand in hand into one of several rustic cabins on Daintree. These cabins were meant to be a temporary place to rest while moving cattle from one grazing spot to another. His grandfather was using them for a much different purpose. Hawk had locked this secret deep inside for many years; he had never told his grandfather what he had seen, and he had never told his grandmother either. To learn that her husband, a man she always praised as being honest and true, was a philanderer would have broken Debra's heart. Hawk never would have done that to her.

"Now, if you'll excuse me," Hawk said, sitting back down, feeling more at home behind the desk than moments before, "I have work to do."

"My love—" Hawk turned the phone around so Jessie could see his view "—look at this sunrise."

"Wow!" Jessie exclaimed. "Stunning."

It was 5:00 a.m. in Queensland and he called Jessie as soon as he had awakened.

Hawk left the balcony and went back into his grandfather's office. It might take years for him to gain full ownership of the office. Frankly, he wasn't certain he would ever have that chance. He was married now; he had a family on the way. Any decision they made about their future had to made together.

"I feel like we've danced around this a couple of times now," Jessie said. "Don't you think it's time we talk about the will?"

Hawk sat down and propped the phone up against a stack of books so he could look at his beautiful wife. "Yes, I do."

Jessie raised her eyebrows, waiting for his next words.

"Grandpa wrapped up Daintree Downs in a box and tied it up with a ten-year bow."

"Meaning?"

"If I move back to the station and work the land

for ten consecutive years, I will inherit Daintree Downs."

"Ten years?"

He nodded. "Yes."

"And if you don't?"

"All of the land—the buildings, the equipment, the cattle, horses—will be held in trust by the state of Queensland."

"And you get nothing?"

"Nothing but the clothes on my back and any personal items," Hawk said. "I don't think the State of Queensland will want my grandmother's old pots and pans."

Jessie seemed stunned; he couldn't blame her. He had felt, and still did to some degree, the exact same way. His wife dropped her head into her hands, and he wished that he wasn't a world away so he could comfort her. She was pregnant, newly married, and their plans for building a home on Sugar Creek land seemed like a lifetime ago.

"What are you thinking?" he asked her.

Jessie shook her head, still in her hands, before she lifted up her head so she could look at him again.

"I'm thinking…" She started and then stopped. After a second ticked by, she began again after swallowing several times, as if her tongue was stuck to the roof of her mouth. "I think that we have to move to Daintree Downs."

"No, Jessie," he said. "We don't *have* to do anything. My grandfather did his best to hog-tie me to this ranch, but I'm a man of free will. If Montana is best for you, best for our daughter, then it's what's best for me."

Jessie kept on shaking her head—little, repetitive shakes. "I couldn't live with myself."

"Jessie."

"No." His wife sounded frustrated, shocked, annoyed and exhausted. "I'm serious, Hawk. I couldn't live with myself. The only answer for us is to move to Daintree Downs."

"And how am I supposed to live with myself knowing now what you will be giving up? What our daughter will be giving up? I can't give her what she has there, Jessie. And I can't stand the thought that one day you will wake up and hate me for what you have to give up."

"She'll get something else," she said. "We'll make it work. And for the record, I could never hate you. My heart beats for you."

"It's a hard life, Jess. A real hard life."

Hawk felt sick to his stomach just thinking about how isolated Jessie might feel at Daintree. Yes, he'd considered it before, but now he had a concrete comparison between Sugar Creek and his cattle station. It would have been so much easier if he had never seen Sugar Creek or experienced for himself how tight knit Jessie's extended family was on their ranch.

"I'm sure it is. But we'll face it together. We'll fight through it together. And through it all, I will have you, Hawk. Right?"

"Yes," he said. "Always."

"Then that's all that really matters to me."

Jessie didn't have a good poker face; what she felt was always reflected in her gaze. It was a relief for him to read in her clear, sapphire blue eyes that she meant what she was saying.

"Is Daintree Downs ideal for me?" Jessie asked rhetorically. "No, I can't lie and say that it is. But *you* are ideal for me. I can adjust to anything as long as I have you."

"Promise you won't resent me?" he asked.

"No way." She teased him with a cheeky wink. "I absolutely reserve the right to resent you! And then we'll fight, and then I'll feel horrible about it, apologize, and then we'll have great makeup sex and start working on baby number two!"

"I just love you, Jess. Do you know that?"

Jessie smiled brightly at him, her eyes full of love. "I do. And I love you. I always want you to know that, Hawk, every second of every day. My heart is full of love for you."

Hawk arrived in Montana three weeks later. When he landed on American soil, he felt at home—not the same as he felt about Australia or Daintree Downs but real and surprising. What wasn't surprising was his absolute joy in seeing Jessie again. Everything and everyone faded into the background when he spotted his love waiting for him. Once she was back in his arms, once he was able to catch the clean, fragrant scent of her silky black hair, once he was able to kiss her soft lips, that was the moment he was able to breathe a sigh of relief. Not even realizing it, Hawk had been living with an undercurrent of anxiety while he was away from Jessie. He had become too accustomed to having her by his side; he couldn't even remember how he had managed to be away from her during the long-distance part of their relationship.

"It's good to be back." Hawk draped his arm over his wife's shoulders.

"Did you miss Montana?" Jessie asked, her arm securely around his waist.

"I did, actually." He smiled at her. "But not nearly as much as I missed you. That was a whole different level."

"Same."

They piled into her car and headed out for Hunter and Skyler's farm. They had a quick meal, an even quicker shower and then slipped into bed and each other's arms. It seemed that Jessie's body had changed so much during the time they were apart, and he regretted it.

After they made love, they lay facing each other, legs intertwined, skin to skin, their fingers threaded together. Jessie's body was so beautiful to him in every stage of her pregnancy; now her breasts were larger, more tender, and her baby bump had turned into a definite baby belly that she proudly showed off to him before they showered.

"You look beautiful, my love." Hawk admired her with his eyes. He drank her in. Her skin was glowing—literally *glowing*—and there was a sparkle in her eyes that had never been there before.

"Thank you," she said, stroking the top of his hand with her thumb. "I've had such a great pregnancy. I feel great, I love the way my body feels…"

"I love the way your body looks *and* feels." Hawk placed his hand on her belly, something he was fond of doing.

"Did you feel that?" Jessie asked, looking down at her belly. "Debra must like the sound of your voice."

Feeling his daughter kicking against his hand was unlike anything he'd ever experienced before. Yes, he had seen the images, and yes, he had felt kicks before. But this was somehow different. It was as if his little girl was sending a message just for him.

All Hawk could do was lean in and kiss his bride. Jessie was giving him the gift of fatherhood. In his early years, he'd never thought much about being a parent; his heart, his mind and his soul were all wrapped tightly around the cattle station.

"Do you think we'll call her Deb? Debbie?" Jessie asked thoughtfully, rubbing her hand over his arm.

"My grandmother went by Deb," he told her.

"Debra Yvonne when she's in trouble."

"We'll be using that a lot, I would imagine."

Jessie laughed. "With American cowgirl and outback rancher in her veins? This little girl is going to be a daredevil wild child who gives us many sleep-less nights."

They both were imagining their little girl in their minds in the silence. Hawk imagined a daughter who was the spitting image of her beautiful mother: black hair, Brand blue eyes, tall, lanky and smart as a whip. From him, he hoped she got some of his grit, deter-mination and love for the Australian outback.

In that moment, when they were talking about their unborn child and their future, Hawk thought it was the perfect moment to give Jessie a little souve-nir he had brought back from Australia.

"Close your eyes, my love," he said. "I have a surprise for you."

"A surprise for me?" Jessie asked with a child-like excitement that he loved. His wife really did like presents.

He nodded. "Close your eyes."

Hawk reached over to open the nightstand drawer, where he had hidden the present. He held the gift in his hand and then asked his wife to open her eyes.

Jessie opened them and stared at the gift in his hand.

"Is that…?"

Hawk smiled at her; it was the first genuine smile he'd had on his face since finding out his grandfa-ther had died. "Yes, it is."

"I can't." His wife shook her head.

"Yes, you can." Hawk took her hand and slipped his grandmother's engagement ring, a two-carat miner's cut diamond set in platinum, onto the ring finger of Jessie's left hand.

"It's beautiful, Hawk," Jessie said. "Truly it is. But I can't wear this knowing that your grandfather didn't want me to have it."

Jessie started to take off the ring, but he stopped her. "My grandfather left this for you in his will."

"He did?"

"He did." Hawk kissed her hand. "He loved you, Jess. This should prove it to you."

Jessie admired the ring on her finger before she kissed him deeply on the lips. "I'll cherish it for the rest of my life, Hawk. I sincerely will."

"I know you will, my love." He folded her into his embrace. "But never as much as I will cherish you."

They had both fallen into an exhausted sleep only to wake up at sundown. Hawk had hesitated to broach the subject of moving to Australia but knew that he had to be sure that Jessie was certain. After they rolled themselves out of bed, they threw a meal together and sat down at the table. At the end of dinner, Hawk asked her, "Daintree Downs. Are you sure?"

"No," she said, and then followed up with "Yes."

"It won't be easy."

"No."

"It's one of the hardest things you'll ever do in your life."

He now knew what Jessie was giving up by leaving Sugar Creek. Yes, on his end, he would be losing thousands of acres and a family legacy, but he wasn't losing his family. There was not enough money in the world to make up for that loss; a family like Jessie's was priceless.

His wife looked at him thoughtfully. "You were going to do it for me."

"Yes." It was true. He had been prepared to give up everything for Jessie and their daughter.

Jessie reached for his hand and squeezed it reassuringly. "Wherever you go, I go."

"Wherever you go, I go." Hawk repeated the sentiment, then he asked, "And what about your horses?"

"I've thought about that," Jessie told him. "I'd like to start a breeding program on Daintree Downs."

"I think that's a brilliant idea, my love. Just brilliant."

For a few seconds, Jessie's eyes focused on something over his shoulder. Then, she brought her eyes back to him. "We have to tell my parents."

He nodded his agreement. "The sooner we do, the better."

"I've stalled them as long as I could," she said. "But I sense that they might have an inkling that something is up."

"We should tell them tomorrow."

Jessie reached for her phone and sent a text to her mother. After a long minute, her phone chimed with a text.

Suddenly, his wife seemed very tired. With a sigh,

she asked, "Do you mind cleaning this up? I really need to lie back down. Your daughter has been kicking me like crazy today."

"Okay, my love."

Hawk followed Jess into the bedroom, helped her out of her clothing and then held back the covers for her to slip into bed. He pulled the sheet and blanket up to her neck and then kissed her sweetly. "Good night, my beautiful wife."

"I love you." She returned his kiss.

"And I love you. Always remember that you are my pride and joy."

"Hawk!" Lilly greeted him with such affection that it settled his nerves a bit. "We're so glad to have you home."

"Thank you," he said and returned her hug. "It feels good to be back."

That was the truth; it did feel good. But this didn't. He knew that the news they were about to share would not be welcome by either of Jessie's parents. And he understood why.

In their minds, the two of them would be building on Sugar Creek, and they would have regular interactions with Debra Yvonne. Instead, he would be taking their only daughter and a grandchild to another continent.

"Hawk." Jock reached out one hand to give him a firm handshake. During the time he had been away, Jock had made some strides in his recovery. His eyes were bright and his skin looked healthy. He even looked as if he had lost a few pounds around the middle.

"Sir," Hawk said with a genuine smile. Jock was a tough old dog, that was for sure, and he was proud to have a man of Jock's caliber as his child's grandfather.

"Let's go to the dining room," Lilly said, linking her arm with Jessie's.

"We weren't really thinking about eating…" Jessie sent a worried glance over her shoulder at Hawk.

Jock walked up behind him and patted him on the back. "Let's belly up, son. Life always looks better on a full stomach."

Chapter Sixteen

Jessie sat next to Hawk at the long family dining table, which had been custom made from wood sourced from Sugar Creek and was large enough to seat their whole family, including spouses. Today, it was just the four of them, a rare moment at the main house when one sibling or another hadn't stopped by for a meal. It felt odd.

"So," Jock said after he wiped his mouth with a cloth napkin, balled it up and threw it on his plate, "fill us in."

Jessie looked at Hawk, who had barely eaten anything; he had picked at some scrambled eggs and plain toast, which Lilly had absolutely noticed.

"We were very sorry to hear about your grandfather, Hawk," Lilly said.

"That's right," Jock added. "We're torn up about it."

"Thank you." Hawk nodded solemnly. "He took me in after my parents died and taught me everything I know about ranching."

"If there's anything we can do, please let us know," Lilly said.

"Thank you," Hawk said for the second time in a short span.

Then came an uncomfortable silence. Jock cocked up one bushy white brow as he looked around the table. "What's going on here? What don't I know?"

"We do have some news," Hawk said slowly. Then he cleared his throat several times loudly before he continued.

In the meantime Jock, always impatient, banged his fist on the table and said, "Lord Jesus, son. Just spit it out! None of us are getting any younger!"

Lilly squeezed her husband's hand and tried her best to be the calming factor, a role she had played from the very beginning of her marriage with Jock.

"My grandfather did not…*approve* of my decision to move to Montana."

Jock scowled at that thought. In his mind, Montana was the closest thing to being in God's presence that a man could get.

"He didn't have anything against Montana, Dad, he just didn't want Hawk to live here," Jessie clarified. "He wanted him to take over Daintree Downs, keep it running for the future generations."

"Well—" Jock softened his expression slightly "—I

can certainly understand that. That's what Brands have going on here with Sugar Creek. I want all my children, my grandchildren and, God willing, my *great*-grandchildren to all be here with us."

"There isn't any easy way to say this," Hawk said, "so I just need to get it out. As a condition of my grandfather's will, in order for me to inherit Daintree Downs, I must live at the cattle station for a period of ten years."

Jock's brow wrinkled; he looked at his wife, then Jessie and then back to Hawk. He leaned forward, resting his forearms on the edge of the table. "Come again?"

Jessie jumped in, "Dad, we have to move to Australia. If we don't, Daintree Downs will be donated to the state of Queensland."

Lilly's face registered shock; Jock's face registered anger. She saw her husband's face turning red, and that brought her back to the most urgent issue: his health.

"Jock Brand." Lilly used a rare tone of voice, one that brooked no argument from any of them, including Jock.

"You're right. You're right," Jock said, shaking his head a bit. "I've got plenty to say, but if I say it, I may blow the lid off this thing, and we might lose touch with our baby girl."

"Then don't say anything right now," Lilly said in a calm, steady tone. To Hawk, she asked, "Is there any way around it?"

"No," Hawk said, "I'm afraid not. I've gotten the best legal advice money can buy."

"It's nearly a million acres of land," Jessie said with a beseeching tone in her voice. "It's Hawk's legacy. But more than that, it's the legacy of his mother's people too. The indigenous people of Australia. No matter how much I—*we*—want to stay here on Sugar Creek, build our house, raise our family—" she caught her husband's eyes and held on to his hand for support "—I can't let him lose Daintree Downs. I just can't. I'd never forgive myself."

"What about the K1 visa?" her mother asked. "The green card?"

"It could take up to a year and half before we got it because there's such a backlog in immigration," Jessie told her. "We don't have that kind of time. The will stipulates that Hawk has six months to settle his affairs and return to the cattle station."

"And the baby?" Lilly asked. "You will still have the baby here, won't you?"

Jessie nodded. "That's the plan. After I have the baby, Hawk will return to Australia. It could be three to six months before the baby could fly internationally. As soon as Debra is ready to make the trip, we will go to Australia."

Jock looked like a balloon that had just been popped; he leaned back in his chair, deflated. It was odd to see her father at a loss for words.

After she thought for a minute, Lilly lifted her chin with confidence, reached for her husband's hand again and nodded her head at them reassuringly. "It's going to be okay. Life is full of tough choices."

"Ten years." Jock's eyes seemed to drift off as if he were looking down an imaginary yardstick of the years ahead.

"They will only be a plane flight away," Lilly said.

"I hate airplanes," Jock groused.

"But you love Jessie more than you hate airplanes. Isn't that true?"

Jock caught her eye. Ever since she was a young girl crawling up into his lap while he worked at his desk, they had shared a special bond.

"I love my baby girl more than I love anything in this world other than you," Jock said to his wife with an emotional waver in his voice. Then he looked at Hawk and said, "I was afraid, right from the start that you were going to take my little girl away from me."

"I know, sir," Hawk said sincerely. "I'm sorry."

"I don't want to hear sorry from you, Bowhill," Jock shot back. "I want to hear that you're going to love her every single day, just like I have."

"I will."

"Cherish her," her father continued, "and keep her safe."

"I promise."

"And never forget—" Jock stabbed the table with his finger "—that my Jessie is the most special little girl in the world."

"You have my word, sir."

Having said his piece, Jock stood up from the

table, turned on his heel and walked stiffly out of the dining room.

"Will he be okay?" Jessie asked her mother, wanting reassurance. She knew that she had just broken her father's heart.

"Jock Brand is the toughest man I know," Lilly said in a clear, steady voice, "and you, my dear, are cut from the exact same cloth. Never forget that."

The day of Callie's wedding was a perfectly sunny Montana day. The sky was a beautiful, expansive shade of aqua blue dotted with a few, billowy clouds. After they had made the difficult decision to live permanently at Daintree Downs *and* they had had the hard talk with her parents, Jessie decided to just rip the Band-Aid off and sent a group text out to her siblings and sisters-in-law sharing the news about the move to Australia after Debra Yvonne was born and get the fallout all at once. That, in Jessie's mind, was better than letting her immediate family know one by one and fielding upset calls over several days.

"I still can't believe you're leaving us," Savannah said, zipping up the back of her champagne-colored gown for her.

"I know." Jessie put her last thank-you note on the top of the pile. "It's still feels so *unreal* to me."

"It won't feel unreal when you're out in the boonies with the kangaroos." Savannah caught herself. "I'm sorry. That was horrible of me."

"It's okay." Jessie spun around. "How do I look?"

"Like a beautiful angel," her sister-in-law said.

Jessie looked at her reflection in the full-length mirror. The bridesmaid dress Callie had chosen for her was perfect for a woman with a baby belly—it was simple and elegant. She actually felt pretty in the dress when lately she had been feeling like she had swallowed an inflatable beach ball. The days of *not* feeling pregnant were over.

"I *am* sorry for that comment," Savannah said. "I just was so excited that our children were going to grow up together right here on the ranch."

"I know." Jessie nodded, her tone of voice reflecting her own disappointment. "I was too."

Savannah reached for her hand. "Are you sure about this, Jess?"

"Hawk asks me the same thing all the time," she replied. "I'm not sure. I don't even know how I'll adjust. But there is one thing that I'm absolutely sure of… I love Hawk. And wherever he is, that's where I have to be."

The church was elegantly decorated with champagne satin ribbons and red roses. Thirty minutes before the start of the wedding, the pews were already filled with friends and family members of the bride and groom.

"I—I feel scared." Callie was standing in front of a full-length mirror, her cheeks flushed with excitement and nervousness.

"That's natural." Kate put her arm around her

daughter's shoulders and smiled at their reflections in the mirror. "Everyone feels that way before they walk down the aisle. Isn't that right, Jessie?"

Jessie took the prized tiara out of the box and brought it over to Kate and Callie. "Absolutely."

Kate took the tiara from Jessie and placed it ever so carefully on top of Callie's hair, which had been swept up into a beautiful bun with tendrils at her temples and down her back.

"Now," Callie's mother said, "you are, without a doubt, the most beautiful bride I have ever seen."

"I—I still feel scared."

"Surely you aren't scared to marry Tony, are you?" Kate asked, concerned.

"No." Callie shook her head. "What if I—I can't say my vows right."

Kate gave a relieved laugh and hugged her daughter. "My wonderful, incredible daughter, you will do just fine."

There was a knock at the door, and Tottie, Tony's mother, poked her head in. "Okay to come in?"

"Yes!" Kate said. "Come in and see Tony's bride."

Tottie came in a flurry of billowy lavender chiffon, her white-blond hair slicked back into a clean chignon, and when she glided into the room, Jessie could smell a faint hint of the mother of the groom's favorite vanilla-honey scent. Tottie gave Jessie a quick hug, then greeted Kate affectionately before she turned all of her attention to the bride.

"Oh, Callie!" Her soon-to-be mother-in-law had

tears of joy in her eyes. "You are a sight to behold. Tony is such a lucky man."

"I—I'm lucky too," Callie said and hid her smile behind her hand. "He's so handsome."

"Well, I can't just stand here blubbering." Tottie gave Kate another hug. "It's almost showtime!"

Not too long after Tottie left, another knock on the door came from Liam. "The pews are full, and Father Paul is ready. Should I give the signal to get started?"

"Are you ready, Callie?" Kate asked.

Callie and Kate exchanged a look befitting the incredible journey of a mother and daughter who refused to let Callie's disability define her potential.

"Yes." Callie nodded definitely, her jitters gone. "I—I'm ready."

Liam gave the signal, and that is when they heard Shane strumming on his acoustic guitar. Callie and Tony hadn't wanted organ music; Callie had always been very certain of this. In her dream wedding, she had always seen her uncle Shane playing his guitar as she walked down the aisle toward the love of her life.

As Callie's maid of honor, technically a *matron* of honor, Jessie was in charge of the train of the dress and the veil. As Callie emerged from her dressing room into the church vestibule, the photographer they had hired began to snap pictures, capturing these precious last moments of her life as a single woman.

Jessie affixed the long crystal-encrusted veil just behind the tiara and then fluffed it out behind the dress. When she finished kneeling down to straighten Callie's train, Jessie was grateful to see Hawk's extended hand to help her up. Her growing belly might make it very difficult to gracefully stand back upright.

Liam held out his arm for Callie to hook hers onto him. He leaned over and said, "I am incredibly proud to have you as my daughter."

Kate took her position at Callie's other side. As she and Liam were walking Callie down the aisle together, Tony's parents, Tony and the rest of the wedding party had made their way down the aisle and taken their seats or their positions at the front of the church.

Once Callie was perfectly situated, Jessie and Hawk stood together waiting their turn to walk down the aisle.

"You do realize that this is the first time we are actually walking down an aisle, Mr. Bowhill?"

"Come to think of it, you're right Mrs. Bowhill." Hawk caught her eye.

"You look mighty handsome in that tuxedo," his wife said.

"And, you look mighty fine in that dress." Hawk smiled down at her in that way that still made her knees feel weak.

While walking down the aisle, Jessie saw the beaming faces of her siblings and their wives. Gabe and Bonita had managed to work their schedules so that they could attend; Colt and Lee had dressed Jock Junior in an adorable toddler tuxedo. A few pews up, Bruce and Savannah made such a lovely couple, with their daughter, Amanda, who had just done an amazing job as flower girl.

"Oh!" Jessie forgot herself when she spotted baby Sawyer sleeping peacefully in his mother's arms. Major Noah Brand was wearing his dress blues and standing beside his beloved wife, Shayna, who looked lovely even with the telltale signs of new-mother no-sleep dark circles beneath her eyes. Noah had his arm around their daughter Isabella's shoulders; Isabella was still holding on to her basket that she had used to throw flowers along with Amanda.

Near the front, Rebecca, Shane's wife, and her two sons from her first marriage, were in attendance. Hunter was there too. Skyler hadn't been able to make it from her treatments, but she had insisted that Hunter fly to Bozeman to support Callie and his family. He had told Jessie earlier that he had a flight booked for the next day to return to New York.

It was a rare occasion that could assemble the eight Brand siblings, significant others and their offspring together in one place. Even though Liam had adopted Callie when she was already an adult, the entire family had taken her into the fold. Everyone wanted to celebrate Callie and Tony's big day, and they turned out as they had never turned out before.

Once Hawk and Jessie took their places with the rest of the wedding party, Shane paused his playing while the wedding guests stood and turned to get the first glimpse of the bride in her dress. There was a noticeable collective intake of breath when Callie, flanked by her parents, appeared in the doorway.

Tony Jr., small in stature, a bit on the portly side, took a handkerchief from his pocket and wiped his eyes when he saw his bride in her gown for the first time.

Slowly, and to the sound of Shane's guitar playing, Callie walked toward her future husband. At the end of the aisle, Callie and her parents stopped and Father Paul asked, "Who gives this woman to be married to this man?"

In unison, Kate and Liam said, "We do."

They both kissed Callie's cheek before Liam had the honor of handing his daughter to Tony. It was a very traditional ritual that Tony and Callie both wanted. Together, arm in arm, Kate and Liam took their place in the front pew on the bride's side of the aisle. On the groom's side, Tottie's husband was holding her tightly, comforting her as she shed tears of relief, joy and sadness.

"You look like a model." Tony Jr. took Callie's hands in his.

"So do you." Callie ducked her head with a pretty blush on her cheeks.

"I love you," Tony Jr. said in a loud whisper.

"I—I love you too."

"Should I kiss you now?"

Callie shook her head with a loud, tinkling laugh. "No. Not yet."

That broke the tension in the room, and many people in the church laughed along with her.

"Just hold on a minute," Father Paul said with a faint smile. "We'll be getting to that part soon enough."

After clearing his throat and waiting for the laughter to die down, Father Paul began the ceremony, "Dearly beloved, we gather here today to witness the joining of Calico and Tony…"

Jessie couldn't believe it, but she did get emotional when Father Paul said, "Tony, you may now kiss your bride."

Tony had a huge grin on his face. He leaned forward and Callie leaned forward, and then, right before he kissed his wife, Tony put up his hand to block the wedding guests from seeing them kiss. After the kiss between Callie and Tony, the congregation erupted in cheers and claps as the newly married bride and groom walked arm in arm up the aisle to an awaiting limousine that would take them to Sugar Creek for the reception.

As the church emptied, Jessie found her husband talking to her brother Shane. Jessie hugged her brother. "You played so beautifully, Shane. You made Callie's dreams come true."

Together, Jessie and Hawk left the church and climbed into her car. Jessie sat behind the wheel but didn't crank the engine.

"Is everything okay?" Hawk asked her.

Jessie looked over at him. "I don't think I've ever

seen—no, I don't think I've ever *witnessed*—anything in my life as incredibly beautiful as this wedding."

"I agree." Her husband nodded. "They had so much stacked against them from Jump Street, and they didn't let anything stop them."

"Yes." Jessie nodded. "I think you've put voice to my feelings. They have inspired me."

Hawk looked out the windshield, mulling over her words, then he looked back at her. "It makes me think that if they can overcome the challenges they've faced, then so can we."

Jessie leaned over for him to kiss her. "Then so can we."

The main house at the ranch was teeming with people. Jessie couldn't remember a time when her parents had hosted anything this large, but then again, Callie had always inspired people to move mountains for her.

Callie had wanted to have an outfit change, and Kate had agreed to it. The wedding guests gathered in preparation for the bride and groom to make their first appearance together as a married couple.

Tony, decked out in a top hat and cane, and Callie, dressed in a tea-length dress with a flouncy skirt and a crystal-encrusted sash, came into the great room to their song "Just the Way You Are" by Bruno Mars. Tony had been practicing for over a year in order to dance the first dance with Callie. His dedication to getting this right only proved to everyone in his life how much he loved her.

Tony took his bride in his arms and, with Callie giggling and laughing, twirled her around in a way that made her skirt fan out around her legs. Jessie saw Kate, standing across the way with Liam, break down. Jessie had never seen Kate cry like that but imagined those tears did not reflect just one emotion. Love, sadness, so much more. Perhaps Kate hadn't really believed that this day would come. But it had. And it had been, and would continue to be, a celebration of true love between two amazing people.

After the couple's first dance, the floor opened up for other couples to join them. Hawk swept Jessie up into his arms and did his best not to step on her toes as he attempted his version of a box-step waltz. After several times of smashing her toes, Jessie thought it would be safer to gather some food and drinks and find their place cards at one of the many tables set up around the dance floor and enjoy the festivities. They found their spot at a table where Lilly and Jock were seated.

"What did you think of the wedding?" Jessie asked her parents.

"Incredible," Lilly said. "Simply incredible."

Her mother put her hand on Jock's shoulder. "Your father actually teared up."

Jock looked completely sheepish but did admit it. "I thought to myself, 'Cracky'—isn't that what you Australian folks say—'this is one hell of a wedding.'"

Jessie's eyes widened. She leaned forward with a very serious sense of urgency and said, "It's *crikey*, Dad! And please don't ever use it again."

Out of the corner of her eye, she could see Hawk grinning broadly. She leaned over, gazing up into her husband's handsome face. "You're just loving this aren't you? You've left your Australian mark on my family!"

Hawk bent his head down, kissed her on the lips and said, "It's fair I should think."

"How do you figure?"

"Because, my love, you and your crazy family have left a very big mark on this outback rancher's heart."

Epilogue

Two years later

"I hear the helicopter!" Jessie shouted to her mother, Lilly, who was puttering around in the kitchen at Daintree Downs.

"Coming!" Lilly called back.

"Daddy and Grandpa are coming, sweet girl." Jessie smiled at Debra Yvonne, who, at eighteen months old, was very steady on her feet and loved to run from one side of the living room to the other. "We're going to have to put on our headphones."

Debra had already taken many helicopter rides with her father, so donning the headphones to protect her ears was second nature to her.

Her daughter laughed happily as she ran over to

Jessie and launched herself forward onto her lap; the girl was already proving to be a chip off *both* blocks. She was fearless, adventurous and loved horses and cows—a true rancher's daughter with a good dose of Montana cowgirl.

"Daddy up!" Debra Yvonne yelled and pointed out the window.

Lilly rushed into the living room, scooped up her granddaughter into her arms and went straight out onto the large veranda.

"I still can't believe that your father gets in the helicopter with Hawk," Lilly said, holding tight to Debra.

"I can't believe how close the two of them have gotten," Jessie mused. "Hawk counts Dad as one of his best friends."

Over the last year, Jock and Lilly had traveled to Australia multiple times, staying for a month each visit. They had started to explore the rest of the continent when they weren't enjoying their time at Daintree Downs. Even though it was, and continued to be, challenging for Jessie to make her life in such a remote place, the fact that her parents regularly visited her had helped her adjust to her new outback life. And, when she wasn't receiving visitors, Jessie had her hands full helping Hawk with management of the cattle station, raising their daughter and building her herd of American quarter horses.

"There's Daddy!" Jessie pointed as the helicopter came into view.

Hawk, who had been flying since he was a young man, skillfully landed the helicopter and turned off the engine. Once it was safe, her dad and her husband got out of the helicopter and headed for the front porch.

"How was it?" Lilly asked Jock, handing Debra over to him.

"By cracky, this ranch is damn near as close to God's country as Sugar Creek," Jock said, bouncing his granddaughter in his arms.

"That's high praise, Dad," Jessie said.

"It certainly is." Lilly smiled at them both.

Hawk joined them on the porch and kissed Jessie on the lips before he asked her, "How are you?"

"Happy to see you." She put her arm around him, her spirits always lifted whenever Hawk came home.

"And—" her husband put his hand on her barely noticeable baby bump "—how is our new little one?"

Jessie smiled broadly at him as they went into the house. "He's happy you're home too."

* * * * *

Try these other great cowboy romances:

Matchmaker on the Ranch
by Marie Ferrarella

Rancher to the Rescue
by Stella Bagwell

Seven Birthday Wishes
by Melissa Senate

Available now from Harlequin Special Edition!

COMING NEXT MONTH FROM

HARLEQUIN

SPECIAL EDITION

#3007 FALLING FOR DR. MAVERICK
Montana Mavericks: Lassoing Love • by Kathy Douglass
Mike Burris and Corinne Hawkins's rodeo romance hit the skids when Mike pursued his PhD. But when the sexy doctor-in-training gets word of Corrine's plan to move on without him, he'll pull out all the stops to kick-start their flatlined romance.

#3008 THE RANCHER'S CHRISTMAS REUNION
Match Made in Haven • by Brenda Harlen
Celebrity Hope Bradford broke Michael Gilmore's heart years ago when she left to pursue her Hollywood dreams. The stubborn rancher won't forgive and forget. But when Hope is forced to move in with him on his ranch—and proximity gives in to lingering attraction—her kisses thaw even the grinchiest heart!

#3009 SNOWBOUND WITH A BABY
Dawson Family Ranch • by Melissa Senate
When a newborn baby is left on Detective Reed Dawson's desk with a mysterious note, he takes in the infant. But social worker Aimee Gallagher has her own plans for the baby...until a snowbound weekend at Reed's ranch challenges all of Aimee's preconceived notions about family and love.

#3010 LOVE AT FIRST BARK
Crimson, Colorado • by Michelle Major
Cassie Raebourn never forgot Aiden Riley—or the way his loss inspired her to become a veterinarian. Now the shy boy is a handsome, smoldering cowboy, complete with bitterness and bluster. It's Cassie's turn to inspire Aiden...with adorable K-9 help!

#3011 A HIDEAWAY WHARF HOLIDAY
Love at Hideaway Wharf • by Laurel Greer
Archer Frost was supposed to help decorate a nursery—not deliver Franci Walker's baby! She's smitten with the retired coast guard diver, despite his gruff exterior. He's her baby's hero...and hers. Will Franci's determined, sunny demeanor be enough for Archer to realize *he's* their Christmas miracle?

#3012 THEIR CHRISTMAS RESOLUTION
Sisters of Christmas Bay • by Kaylie Newell
Stella Clarke will stop at nothing to protect her aging foster mother. But when sexy real estate developer Ian Steele comes to town with his sights set on her Victorian house, Stella will have to keep mistletoe and romance from softening her hardened holiday reserve!

HSECNM0823

Get 3 FREE REWARDS!

We'll send you 2 FREE Books plus a FREE Mystery Gift.

FREE Value Over **$20**

Both the **Harlequin® Special Edition** and **Harlequin® Heartwarming™** series feature compelling novels filled with stories of love and strength where the bonds of friendship, family and community unite.

HARLEQUIN PLUS

Try the best multimedia subscription service for romance readers like you!

Read, Watch and Play.

Experience the easiest way to get the romance content you crave.

Start your **FREE TRIAL** at
www.harlequinplus.com/freetrial.